"Stay," sh

He touched ~~a~~ ~~fing~~ and tipped her face up to his. "~~You bel~~ in me that much," he murmured, "because of what we were to each other."

He knew touching her was a mistake the moment his fingertip connected with her soft skin. First, because of the warmth that spread up his arm and lodged in his chest, threatening to undo all his best intentions. And second because her eyes snapped dark with what he thought was fury, but was wiped away before he could be sure, to be replaced by cool, studied indifference. She eased away.

"Despite the impression you might have gotten from my kissing you last night, I'm all too aware of our history. Trusting you got me a broken heart before. This time it could very well put my life in danger."

JESSICA ANDERSEN

INTERNAL AFFAIRS

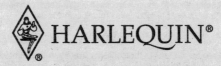

TORONTO • NEW YORK • LONDON
AMSTERDAM • PARIS • SYDNEY • HAMBURG
STOCKHOLM • ATHENS • TOKYO • MILAN • MADRID
PRAGUE • WARSAW • BUDAPEST • AUCKLAND

Recycling programs
for this product may
not exist in your area.

ISBN-13: 978-0-373-69431-0

INTERNAL AFFAIRS

Copyright © 2009 by Dr. Jessica S. Andersen

ABOUT THE AUTHOR

Though she's tried out professions ranging from cleaning sea lion cages to cloning glaucoma genes, from patent law to training horses, Jessica is happiest when she's combining all these interests with her first love: writing romances. These days she's delighted to be writing full-time on a farm in rural Connecticut that she shares with a small menagerie and a hero named Brian. She hopes you'll visit her at www.JessicaAndersen.com for info on upcoming books, contests and to say hi!

Books by Jessica Andersen

*Bear Claw Creek Crime Lab

CAST OF CHARACTERS

Dr. Sara Whitney—As the youngest chief medical examiner in the city's history, and a woman, Sara has political pressure coming from all sides, not to mention that Bear Claw is in the grips of an increasing terrorist threat. When Sara's ex returns from the dead with no memory of where he's been or what he's done, she'll have to put her career, her heart and eventually her life on the line to help him.

Detective Romo Sampson—When his memories begin to return, Romo must face his own past in order to defeat the terrorist threat and reclaim the woman he had loved...and betrayed.

Al-Jihad—A terrorist leader who has plans for Bear Claw Creek.

Jane Doe—The former head of a supersecret covert group, she is now allied with Al-Jihad. Her network of spies runs deep within local and federal law enforcement.

Percy Proudfoot—The acting mayor will do whatever it takes to oust Sara from her position as head ME of Bear Claw Creek.

Jonah Fairfax—The former undercover operative worked for Jane Doe and helped Al-Jihad escape from prison. Can Sara and Romo trust him when things get bad?

Tucker McDermott, Alyssa McDermott, Seth Varitek, Cassie Dumont-Varitek and Chelsea Swan—Sara's friends are a tightly knit group. How far can she push them for help without revealing the truth about Romo's return?

Chapter One

The pain speared from his shoulder blade to his spine and down—raw, bloody agony that consumed him and made him want to sink back into unconsciousness. But at the same time, urgency beat through him, not letting him return to oblivion.

The mission, the mission, must complete the mission.

But what was the mission? Where was he? What the hell had happened to him?

Cracking his eyes a fraction, careful not to give away his conscious state if he was being watched, he surveyed his immediate surroundings. Tall pine trees reached up to touch the late summer sky on all sides of him, their bases furred with an underlayer of smaller scrub brush. There was no sign of a cabin or a road, no evidence of anyone else nearby, no tracks in the forest litter but his own, leading to where he'd collapsed.

He was wearing heavy hiking boots, dark jeans and a black T-shirt, all of which were spattered with blood. Something told him not all of it was his, though when he moved his arms, the agony in his right shoulder ripped a groan from his lips. He felt the warm, wet bloom of fresh blood, smelled it on the moist air.

Shot in the back, he knew somehow. *Bastards. Cowards.* Except that he didn't know who the bastardly cowards were, or why they'd gone after him. More, he didn't know who the hell *he* was. Or what he'd done.

The realization brought a sick chill rattling through him, a spurt of panic. His brain answered with *I've got to get up, get moving. I can't let them catch me, or I'm dead.*

The words had no sooner whispered in his mind than he heard the sounds of pursuit: the sharp bark of a dog and the terse shouts of men calling to one another.

They weren't close, but they weren't far enough away for comfort, either.

He struggled to his feet cursing with pain, staggering with shock and blood loss. He didn't know who was looking for him, but there was far too much blood for a bar fight, and the pattern was high velocity. Had he killed someone? Been standing nearby when someone was killed? Had he escaped from a bad situation, or had he *been* the bad situation?

He didn't know, damn it. Worse, he didn't know which answer he was hoping for.

The mission. The words seemed to whisper from nowhere and everywhere at once. They came from the trees and the wind high above, and the bark of a second dog, sharper this time, and excited, suggesting that the beast had hit on a scent trail.

One thing was for certain: he needed to get someplace safe. But where? And how?

Knowing he wasn't going to find the answer standing

there, bleeding, he got moving, putting one foot in front of the other, holding his right arm clutched against his chest with his left. The world went gray-brown around the edges and his feet felt very far away, but the scenery moved past him, slow at first, then faster when he hit a downhill slope.

He saw a downed tree with an exposed root ball, thought he recognized it, though he didn't know from when. His feet carried him away from it at an angle, as though his subconscious knew where the hell he was going when his conscious mind didn't have a clue. Urgency propelled him—not just from the continued sounds of pursuit, which was drawing nearer by the minute, but also from the sense that he was supposed to be doing something crucial, critical.

His breath rasped in his lungs and the gray-brown closed in around the edges of his vision. He tripped and staggered, tripped again and went down. But he didn't stay down. He dragged himself up again, levering his body with his good arm and biting his teeth against the pained groans that wanted to rip from his throat.

Instead, staying silent, he forced himself to move faster, until he was running downhill through trees that all looked the same. He saw nothing except forest and more forest. Then, in the distance, there was something else: a rectangular blur that soon resolved itself into the outline of a late-model truck parked in the middle of nowhere.

Excitement slapped through him, driving back some of the gray-brown. He didn't recognize the truck, but he'd run right to it, hadn't he? It stood to reason that was because he'd known it was there. More, when he'd climbed into the driver's seat, he automatically fumbled beneath the dashboard and came up with the keys.

It took him two tries to get the key in the ignition; he was wobbly and weak, and he couldn't lean back into the seat without his shoulder giving him holy hell. But he had wheels. A hope of escape.

He couldn't hear the dogs over the engine's roar, but he knew the searchers were behind him, knew the net was closing fast. More, he knew he didn't have much more time left before he lapsed unconscious again. He'd lost blood, and God only knew what was going on inside him. Every inhalation was like breathing flames; every exhalation a study in misery. He needed a place to crash and he needed it fast.

After that, he thought, glancing in the rearview mirror and seeing piercing green eyes in a stern face, short black hair, and nothing familiar about any of it, *I'm going to need some answers.*

Knowing he was already on borrowed time, he hit the gas and sent the truck thundering downhill. There wasn't any road or track, but he got lucky—or else he knew the way—and didn't hit any big ditches or dead-falls. Within ten minutes, he came to a fire-access road. Instinct—or something more?—had him turning uphill rather than down. A few minutes later, he bypassed a larger road, then took a barely visible dirt trail that par-alleled the main access road.

The not-quite-a-road was bumpy, jolting him back against the seat and wringing curses from him every time he hit his injured shoulder. But the pain kept him conscious, kept him moving. And when he hit a paved road, it reminded him he needed to get someplace he could hide, where he'd be safe when he collapsed.

Animalistic instinct had him turning east. He passed street signs he recognized on some level, but it wasn't until he passed a big billboard that said *Welcome to Bear Claw Creek* that he knew he was in Colorado, and then only because the sign said so.

His hands were starting to shake, warning him that his body was hitting the end of its reserves. But he still had enough sense to ditch the truck at the back of a commuter lot, where it might not be noticed for a while, and hide the keys in the wheel well. Then he searched the vehicle for anything that might clue him in on what the hell was going on—or, failing that, who the hell he was.

All he came up with was a lightweight waterproof jacket wedged beneath the passenger's seat, but that was something, anyway. Though the fading day was still warm with late summer sun, he pulled on the navy blue jacket so if anyone saw him, they wouldn't get a look at his back. A guy wearing dirty jeans and a jacket might be forgotten. A guy bleeding from a bullet wound in his shoulder, not so much.

Cursing under his breath, using the swearwords to let him know he was still up and moving, even as the gray-brown of encroaching unconsciousness narrowed his vision to a tunnel, he stagger-stepped through the commuter car lot and across the main road. Cutting over a couple of streets on legs that were rapidly turning to rubber, he homed in on a corner lot, where a neat stone-faced house sat well back from the road, all but lost behind wild flowering hedges and a rambler-covered picket fence.

It wasn't the relative concealment offered by the big lot and the landscaping that had him turning up the driveway, though. It was the sense of safety. This wasn't his house, he knew somehow, but whose ever it was, instinct said they would shelter him, help him.

Without conscious thought, he reached into the brass, wall-mounted mailbox beside the door, found a small latch and toggled the false bottom, which opened to reveal a spare key.

He was too far gone to wonder how he'd known to do that, too out of it to remember whose house this was. It was all he could do to let himself in and relock the door once he was through. Dropping the key into his pocket, he dragged himself through a pin-neat kitchen that was painted cream and moss with sunny yellow accents and soft, feminine curtains. He found a notepad beside the phone and scrawled a quick message.

His hands were shaking; his whole body was shaking, and where it wasn't shaking it had shut down completely. He couldn't feel his feet, couldn't feel much of anything except the pain and the dizziness that warned he was seconds away from passing out.

Finally, unable to hold it off any longer, he let the gray-brown win, let it wash over his vision and suck him down into the blackness. He was barely aware of staggering into the next room and falling, hardly felt the pain of landing face-first on a carpeted floor. He knew only that, for the moment at least, he was safe.

Chapter Two

Chief Medical Examiner Sara Whitney's day started out badly and plummeted downhill from there.

It wasn't just that her coffeemaker had finally gone belly-up. She'd known it was on its last legs, after all, and simply kept forgetting to upgrade. Sort of like how she kept forgetting to replace her anemic windshield wipers because they only annoyed her when it was raining. Or how she hadn't yet gotten around to having the maintenance crew that served the Bear Claw ME's office fix her office door, which stuck half the time and randomly popped open the other half.

No, it wasn't those petty, mundane, *normal* irritations that had her amber-colored eyes narrowed with frustration as she worked her way through her sixth autopsy of the day, dictating her notes into the voice-activated minirecorder clipped to the lapel of the blue lab coat she wore over neatly tailored, feminine pants and a soft blue-green shirt that accented the golden highlights in her shoulder-length, honey-colored hair.

No, what annoyed her was the memo she'd gotten

from Acting Mayor Proudfoot's people, turning down yet another request to hire new staff, even though she'd only proposed to replace two of the three people she'd lost over the past year—two to the terrorist attacks that had gripped the city in the wake of a nearby jailbreak, one to the FBI's training program. What annoyed her further was the knowledge that she was going to have to work yet another twelve-hour day to catch up with the backlog. It didn't help that her three remaining staffers—receptionist Della Jones, ME Stephen Katz, and their newly promoted assistant, Bradley Brown— were all taking their lunch breaks glued to the TV in the break room, with the police scanner cranked to full volume as they followed the manhunt that was unfolding in Bear Claw Canyon, not half an hour away.

Sara didn't want to think about the manhunt, or the fact that the combined Bear Claw PD/FBI task force had lost two men in an op gone bad, leading to the manhunt. She didn't want to think ahead to those autopsies, and felt guilty for hoping the dead men weren't any of the cops or agents she knew. She also didn't want to think about the fact that until terrorist mastermind al-Jihad and his followers were brought to justice, people in and around Bear Claw were going to keep dying.

She didn't want to think about it, but she had to, because it was happening even as she stood there, elbow-deep in the abdominal cavity of an overweight, chain-smoking sixty-three-year-old man whose badly clogged arteries suggested an all too common cause of death. The autopsy was routine, but the events transpiring outside Sara's familiar cinder block world were anything but.

Bear Claw City was at war.

It had been nearly ten months since al-Jihad had managed to escape from the ARX Supermax Prison north of Bear Claw Creek, gaining freedom along with two of his most trusted lieutenants. Since then, it had become clear that al-Jihad's network was deeply entrenched in Bear Claw, twining through both local and federal law enforcement.

Each time a conspirator was uncovered and neutralized, new evidence surfaced indicating that the internal problems extended even further, and that al-Jihad was continuing to unfold an elaborate, devastating plan that the task force just couldn't seem to get a handle on. The cops and agents had uncovered pieces and hints, but the terrorists' main goal continued to elude them, even as the groundswell of suspicious activity seemed to suggest that an attack was imminent.

Of course, the general population knew only some of what was going on. Sara knew more than most because her office was intimately involved with the BCCPD, and because she was close friends with a tightly knit group of cops and agents, three couples plus her as a spare wheel.

The seven friends had banded together the previous year when FBI trainee Chelsea Swan—though back then she'd been one of Sara's medical examiners—had fallen in with FBI agent Jonah Fairfax. Fax had assisted in the jailbreak in his role as a deep undercover operative, only to learn in the devastating aftermath that his superior was a traitor and he'd been unknowingly working on al-Jihad's behalf. Sara, Chelsea, Fax and the others had managed to foil al-Jihad's next planned attack, but they'd only managed to capture one of the terrorists, Muhammad Feyd, who'd proven to be a loyal soldier and had defied all efforts to get him talking.

Al-Jihad and his remaining lieutenant, Lee Mawadi, along with Fax's former boss, the eponymous Jane Doe, remained at large even now, ten months later. In that interim, there had been other, smaller incidents, along with a deadly riot at the ARX Supermax. Which Sara so wasn't thinking about right now.

She didn't want to remember the men who'd died in the riot, or the one man in particular whose death had hit her far harder than it should have.

Focus, girl, she told herself. *The day's only getting longer the more you stall.*

Concentrating on the innards at hand, Sara went through the process by rote, weighing and sampling, dictating notes as she worked. But although the actions were automatic—they ought to be, after six years on the job, two heading the Bear Claw ME's office—they weren't without compassion. Sara's top-flight surgeon mother might consider her daughter's medical skills wasted on the dead, but Sara knew she worked for the families as much as the corpses, and took satisfaction from providing answers, shedding light onto causes of death that might otherwise be misinterpreted.

Contrary to what some popular TV shows might portray, only a small fraction of the bodies coming through the ME's office were instances of foul play. The vast majority was made up of an almost equal balance between natural causes and accidental fatalities. Her current case fell into the former, i.e., a catastrophic cardiac event brought on by a high-risk lifestyle and inconsistently treated hypertension.

As she stripped off her protective gear and headed for her office to finish up the necessary paperwork, Sara found herself wishing that more of her recent cases had been so straightforward. It wasn't that she wanted her life to be easy or boring, but she'd gone into pathology because she'd grown up a passenger of her parents' roller-coaster ride of emotions, and she hadn't wanted the highs and lows of living medicine.

Little had she known she'd wind up in the middle of a terror threat that had the entire city by the throat, and that she'd be far more enmeshed in the case than she would've preferred. Granted, the investigation had moved away from her office in the months since the prison riot, but her close ties to members of the task force kept her involved, as did the caseload she'd been forced to assume in the face of a serious manpower shortage.

The lack of staff members in the ME's office was yet another of Acting Mayor Proudfoot's unsubtle efforts to get rid of all the young, energetic hires made by his forward-thinking predecessor, who had been disgraced and ousted when damning photographs had surfaced involving the mayor and several girls of questionable age.

That had been too bad as far as Sara was concerned; she didn't condone the former mayor's ethical lapses, but she thought he'd been taking the city in a positive direction by bringing fresh blood into the crime scene unit, the ME's office and several other tech-based divi-

sions of city government. Since the ex-mayor's depar-
ture, Proudfoot had been undoing those advances, piece
by piece, making no bones about the fact that he
intended to return Bear Claw Creek to the "good old
days"—i.e., the days of minimal technology and pay-
to-play politics.

Proudfoot's efforts had been blunted somewhat by
the terrorist threat, but his image lurked at the back of
Sara's mind on a daily basis. She knew he was just
waiting for her to mess up badly enough that he could
get rid of her and return the ME's office to the age of
dinosaurs, with his cronies in charge.

"Which is another thing that belongs in the category
of 'things I don't want to think about right now,'" she
said to herself on a long sigh, pinching the bridge of her
nose to stave off the headache that always encroached
when she thought about all the things she was trying not
to think about these days.

The list was long. And frankly, it didn't leave her
much *to* think about.

"Hey, boss." The hail came from Stephen, the sole
remaining medical examiner beside herself. He was
tall, lean and graying, a good ten years older than her
own thirty-five, and had worked in the Bear Claw
ME's office for nearly a dozen years. Miraculously,
though, he didn't seem to resent that Sara—young,
female, relatively inexperienced—had been hired in
above him as his boss. If anything, he seemed happy
to let her have the headaches that came with the
position.

"Hey yourself." Sara didn't ask about the manhunt,

didn't want to know. "You're headed out early today, right?"

He nodded, a soft smile touching his lips, lighting his usual neutral expression. "Celia and I are bringing Chrissy for a checkup." Chrissy was the change-of-life baby, nearly twenty years younger than their eldest, who had surprised Stephen and his wife the year before. By all indications, little Chrissy would grow up dearly beloved by their entire extended family, and most likely spoiled rotten.

The quiet joy on the older man's face squeezed at Sara's heart. She nodded, forcing herself to feel happy for him rather than sorry for herself. "Tell Celia I said hi."

"I'll do that. I can come back after, if you want me to." He glanced at the wipe board that hung in the hallway opposite their office doors, where the pending cases were listed. "Things are backing up."

They were, indeed, and a large part of Sara wanted to keep the office running around the clock until they'd cleared the board and gotten ahead of the looming mountains of paperwork. But logic said that Proudfoot wouldn't be impressed with that show of efficiency. If anything, he'd take it as an indication that she'd manage just fine with an even smaller staff.

She shook her head. "Thanks for the offer, but no. Head on home. I'll clear what I can, and we can start over tomorrow."

He sent her a long look. "Promise me you won't stay past normal human quitting time? It *is* Friday. You know…the weekend?"

She winced. "You got me. We'll start over on Monday." Which didn't mean she wouldn't be in over the next two days. She had abolished the weekend and overnight shifts due to staff constraints, but she still liked to come into the office herself, when everything was relatively quiet.

Two years earlier, it would've been easy to promise Stephen she'd leave for the weekend, because she would've known there was someone waiting for her at home—someone to cook with, eat with, laugh with, love with.

Even a year ago, having more or less recovered from the catastrophic implosion of that relationship, she would've had plans of some sort. She and Chelsea would've hooked up with Cassie Dumont-Varitek and Alyssa McDermott, their friends in the BCCPD crime scene unit, and had a girls' night out. Or maybe they would've "double dated," with Cassie and Alyssa pairing up with their husbands, while Chelsea and Sara hung together.

It wasn't the same these days with Chelsea gone into the FBI training program on the East Coast, though. Sara had tried going out with the others, and had felt like a fifth wheel. Chelsea had been the glue holding them together. Without her, it felt as if the rest of them were trying too hard. Even when Chelsea and Fax came back to the city, they were most often there on task force business, maybe with a little wedding planning snuck in on the side.

Things had changed. The others had moved on, leaving Sara behind.

Summoning a smile, she waved Stephen away. "Go on, get moving. You wouldn't want to keep your women waiting."

But he didn't move. Instead, he gave her a long, intense look. "I'll do the agents when they come in, if you'd like. I can be here tomorrow morning, assuming they release the bodies that early."

He was talking about the manhunt, the men who'd died. She closed her eyes, feeling guilty over the stab of relief brought by the offer. "Have they announced the names?"

"Not yet."

She nodded, knowing that even though she hadn't been paying attention to the reports, the knowledge of the deaths, and the echoes it brought, had permeated her. "I'll let you know." Which was as close as she was going to get to confessing that she couldn't handle how close the terrorists were hitting, and how much it bothered her that things seemed to be ramping up rather than settling down these days. It was hard not to wonder where it would all stop, and how many would die in the attack most of the task force members thought was imminent.

Her mother and father were in rare agreement that she should give notice and get the hell out of Bear Claw Creek. Sara had seriously considered the option…for about thirty seconds before coming to the realization that she couldn't do it. This was her home; she wasn't giving up on it. And what was more, she wasn't walking away from her job or her remaining staff members.

This was her department, damn it. She might be going down, but she was going down fighting.

After another long look, Stephen headed out. Telling herself she appreciated his concern, that it didn't make her feel even lonelier than she had before, Sara completed the necessary paperwork on the cases she'd autopsied so far that day, then suited back up and returned to work.

She processed three more routine cases over the remainder of the day and did her best to tune out the news bulletins when she passed through the break room, or got near Della's desk, where the fiftysomething admin assistant had a police band radio turned low. Still, Sara couldn't avoid knowing that the senior agents had called off the op, that the search dogs had followed two different trails ascribed to the terrorists, both of which had dead-ended in vehicle tracks heading for the main roads.

It seemed that the op had been a quick scramble into the state forest, based on intel that several of al-Jihad's people were holed up in a remote cabin, strategizing. Sara didn't want to know but couldn't help hearing that the two agents had lost their lives in pursuit of a small knot of men who appeared to have been carrying bodies, while a lone man had escaped in the opposite direction, and vanished into the wind. She didn't want to know that the cabin had been stripped bare, and had burst into flames within minutes of the terrorists' escape, torched by a hidden incendiary device.

As usual, al-Jihad's people had been well prepared. Sara wasn't sure what the op had aimed to do, or what the terrorists had planned or accomplished in the forest, but she knew the names of the dead men now, whether she wanted to or not. Both FBI agents, they weren't among her friends or acquaintances, but they'd had their own friends and families, their own loved ones who'd been cruelly left behind. More bereaved to add to the list that had grown over the past ten months.

Sadness beat through Sara as she kept working, starting another case because it wasn't as though she had any pressing reason to go home, Friday night or not.

Della and Bradley clocked out around five-thirty and left arm in arm. Bradley had been mooning after Della—who was a good decade his senior and the mother of two grown children—for as long as he'd been working there. Sara smiled, her heart warming at seeing them so obviously together, though she found herself wondering how she'd missed that change in relationship status. Then she had to remind herself not to dwell on the fact that everyone around her seemed to be pairing up these days. Everyone but her.

Biting back a sigh, she got back to work. By the time she called it a night, around 7:00 p.m., her shoulders, back and neck were burning from the strain. She would've killed for a massage, or at least an hour in a whirlpool, but she couldn't bring herself to hit the gym this late on a Friday.

There was a fine line between being single and being pathetic.

Consoling herself with the thought of a long, hot bath, she collected her hybrid from the parking lot, which was located between the BCCPD's main station house and the connected building that held the ME's office.

The twenty-minute drive home was an easy one, and

the sight of the small stone-faced house eased something inside her, even in the darkness.

She'd fallen in love with the place on her first drive through the city. The cottagelike house had been way out of her budget, but she'd taken an uncharacteristic leap and bought it on an adjustable mortgage, then switched over to a fixed loan as soon as she was able to afford the higher payments. These days she was managing the expenses, though there wasn't much left over at the end of the month for extras or savings. She didn't regret the purchase for a second, though. It was her home, plain and simple.

The house was easily big enough for two people—hell, for a small family—but she'd resisted the option of taking on a roommate because she liked to keep her space the way she liked it, with none of the rapid changes she'd endured during childhood. The one person she'd shared her home with—albeit for only a few months—had fit into her world so seamlessly, despite their obvious differences, that she'd thought it would last. It hadn't, of course. And the final words between them had been angry ones.

"Stop it," she told herself as she parked the hybrid near the house, then gathered her bag and coat to head for the kitchen door.

She didn't know why her ex was so much in her mind lately, but enough was enough. He wasn't coming back, and they hadn't been together for the year prior to the prison riot that had taken his life. His death had been tragic, but it didn't magically erase his sins, didn't erase his betrayal. Not by a long shot.

Muttering under her breath, she fished in her bag for her keys, unlocked the door and let herself through. Two steps into the kitchen, with the door swinging shut at her back, she stopped dead as the smell of blood tickled her nostrils. It was a familiar odor, of course, but it wasn't one that belonged in her house.

She stayed frozen for a moment, adrenaline kicking her heart into overdrive.

Logic said she should get out of the house, get somewhere safe and call for help. But something she couldn't name—anger at the growing suspicion that an intruder had broken in, maybe, or a complete and utter lapse of her usual good judgment—had her flicking on the lights and moving farther into the house.

She didn't see anything out of place in her pretty kitchen, but the back of her neck prickled, warning her that someone had been there who shouldn't have been. Holding her breath, she eased through the doorway connecting the kitchen to the living room. And froze in horror.

A man lay on the floor beside her sofa, blood soaking the carpet beneath him.

Sara stifled a scream, swallowing it in a bubble of hysteria. Her saner self said, *Run! Get the hell out of here!* But something had her stalling in place as her heart hammered in her chest.

Her brain racked up impressions in quick succession: the big man lay motionless, but he was breathing. He wore jeans, a dark blue jacket and boots with soil and gravel embedded in the treads. She could see their bottoms because he lay on his face, hands outstretched, one nearly touching a pen and notepad as though he'd dropped them when he fell.

Her panicked brain replayed info from the radio bulletins: a group of men had disappeared in one direction, carrying a couple of bodies. A single man had gone off alone. Having spent the day listening to snippets about the dead agents and the unsuccessful manhunt in the forests of Bear Claw Canyon State Park, Sara knew damn well she should be running for her life, screaming her head off, doing something, *anything* other than standing there, gaping. But she didn't move. She stayed rooted in place, staring at the notepad.

She knew that writing.

Emotion grabbed her by the throat, choking her and making her heart race even as logic told her it was impossible. That wasn't his writing. Couldn't be. The man lying there, bleeding, was a stranger. A danger. *Get out of the house,* she told herself. *You're imagining things.*

But she didn't run. She edged around the man and leaned down to read the note. It said: *Nobody can know that I'm here. Life or death.*

Sara reached for the notepad, then stopped herself. Her hand was shaking and tears tracked down her cheeks unheeded.

"No," she whispered, the single word hanging longer than it should have in the silence. "He's dead."

But she knew that writing, had seen it on countless notes tucked under her coffee mug, or left beside the phone, telling her where he was going, when he'd be back, or that he'd pick up dinner on the way. Love notes, she'd liked to think them, even though he'd never said those exact words.

Hope battered against what she knew to be true. *He's dead,* she thought. *I went to his funeral.*

Yet she reached out trembling fingers to touch thick, wavy black hair that was suddenly, achingly familiar. And stopped herself.

All rational thought said she should call for help. The note, though, said not to. She wouldn't have hesitated, except for the damn writing. It was shaky, but it was his. She'd swear to it.

She could turn him over and prove it one way or the other. It wasn't as if he was going anywhere fast. He was out cold, his back rising and falling in breaths so shallow they were almost invisible. Blood soaked the rug beneath him; the smell of it surrounded him.

Sara's inner medical professional sent a stab of warning as she dithered on one level, assessed his injuries on another. *He's pale, probably shocky. If you don't do something soon, it won't matter who he is because he'll be dead.*

"Call 9-1-1," she told herself. "Don't be an idiot."

Instead, she reached out and touched him—his stubble-roughened cheek first, then the pulse at his throat. As she did so, she tried to get a sense of his profile, tried to see if it was—

No. It couldn't be.

Yet her heart sped up, her head spun and her breath went thin in her lungs as she debated between checking his spine—which was the proper thing to do before moving him—and turning his face so she could see, so she'd know for sure.

Then he groaned—a low, rough sound—and said something unintelligible in a voice that was achingly familiar. Heat raced through her. Hope.

He moved his right arm and let out another groan of pain. Then, as though sensing that she was there, he shifted, snaking out his left hand to grab her ankle—not hard, more looping his fingers around her, touching but not restricting her.

Sara squeaked and would have jerked away, but once again she was frozen in place, paralyzed by the memory of a lover who'd kept a careful distance between them when awake, but in sleep had always wanted some part of him touching some part of her, as though reassuring himself she was still there.

"Romo?" she whispered. The single word burned her lips and hurt her chest.

Then he shifted again, this time turning his face toward her, so she saw him in profile against the bloodied carpet.

Her throat closed on a noise that might've been a cross between a scream and a moan if it had made it past the lump jamming her windpipe. As it was, the cry reverberated in her head.

She knew that profile—the clean planes of his nose and brow; the dark, elegant eyebrows; the angular jaw. If he was awake and smiling—or snarling, for that matter—at her, she would've known his square, regular teeth and the glint in his dark green eyes. It was really him, she realized, her chest aching with the force of holding back the sobs.

Detective Romo Sampson. Internal affairs investigator. Live-in lover-turned-nemesis. And a dead man back from the dead.

Chapter Three

In that first moment of recognition, Sara's brain threatened to overload with shock and an awful, undeniable sense of hope. She wanted to scream, wanted to laugh, wanted to shriek, "What the hell is going on here? Where have you been? What have you been doing? Why did you let us—let *me*—think you were dead?"

Instead, she forced herself to do what she did best—she buried her emotions, smoothing out the roller coaster.

Clicking over to doctor mode, she shoved her feelings aside, bundling them up along with all the questions that echoed inside her skull. Where had he been for the past four months? What had happened to him? Whose grave had she stood over, dry-eyed but grieving? Whose blood was spattered on his face, arms and hands? It wasn't all his, that was for sure.

He couldn't answer those questions now, though, and might not ever be able to unless she worked fast. Instinct told her he was close to dying a second time.

Sara's heart stuttered a little when she cataloged Romo's injuries and vitals. His breathing was too shallow, the pulse at his throat too slow. And his eyes, when she peeled back his lids, were fixed, the pupils unequal in size, indicating a concussion, or worse.

Shock, she thought, *head injury, and…* She checked him over without rolling him, hissing in a breath when she zeroed in on the wet seep of blood beneath the jacket. *A gunshot wound.*

The hole was ragged at the edges, indicating that the bullet hadn't been going full power when it hit him, and the bruise track suggested it had deflected off his shoulder blade and done more damage to his trapezius muscle than his skeleton. The skin around the injury was inflamed and angry, the blood clotted in some places, still seeping in others. She pressed on his back near the wound, digging into the lax muscles on either side of his spine, hoping the bullet had stayed close to the surface, praying it hadn't fragmented and deflected into vital organs.

He groaned in obvious pain, but didn't move. His hand had fallen away from her ankle, as though having made that effort he'd lapsed more deeply unconscious.

She couldn't find the bullet, but confirmed that his reflexes were decent in his legs, and, having removed his boots, his feet. Her brain spun. The basic exam didn't indicate an immediate spine injury, but the bullet could lie near the vital areas, poised to shift and impinge on the critical nerves if she made a wrong move. She needed more information, needed an X-ray, needed— hell, she needed a doctor who had more experience with living tissue than dead, one who wasn't faintly unnerved to feel warmth beneath her fingertips.

The heat of him, so unlike the refrigerated flesh she touched on a daily basis, unsettled her. More, it wasn't just any living body. It was Romo's living body, which should've been impossible.

Where the hell have you been? she wanted to shout at him. *How could you let everyone think you were dead?*

By "everyone" she meant herself and his parents, because while the funeral had been well attended, and dozens of cops, agents and other staffers had railed against the prison riot that had taken his life, as far as she'd been able to tell, she had been one of the few who had truly mourned his death, one of the few who'd truly considered him a friend, even after everything that had happened between them.

His parents had been there. They'd been shattered and disbelieving, and Sara hadn't had the strength to say anything to them, hadn't wanted to try to define her non-relationship with their son. And maybe she hadn't wanted to admit that she'd been grieving more for what she and Romo'd had in the past, for the man she'd thought him, not the man he'd turned out to be.

Who, apparently, was alive, though not well.

Crouched beside him, one hand on his warm, blood-soaked shoulder, Sara fought an inner battle. She should call for an ambulance, get him to the hospital. The surgeons could deal with the bullet, the cops with his fate. She didn't owe him anything.

But instead of reaching for the phone, she picked up his note and scanned it a second time. *Nobody can know that I'm here.* That was straightforward enough, though difficult under the circumstances, when she needed to get him to an ER. *Life or death*. But whose life or death. Hers? His? A larger threat?

Prior to his death—or what she'd thought was his death—Romo had been working with the BCCPD and occasionally the FBI, using his undeniable computer skills in an effort to ferret out the suspected terrorist conspirators within the BCCPD. Though he'd set his sights on Sara's office as the center of the conspiracy—no doubt thanks in part to Proudfoot's influence—Romo had also been looking at other departments, other cops. Then he'd been killed—supposedly—in the prison riot.

The rumors had said his death had been no accident, that he'd been getting too close to the conspirators and they'd managed to take him out.

From there, Sara realized, it was a short leap to believing that his apparently faked death was related to the case, too. What if he'd used it to drop under deep cover? Chelsea's fiancé, Fax, had pretended to be a killer in order to get himself incarcerated in the ARX Supermax, in an effort to get close to al-Jihad. It was certainly possible that Romo, though a detective rather than an agent, had done something similar. If she assumed he was the lone man who'd escaped the net of the manhunt, then maybe he'd fled the terrorists because they'd found him out, or betrayed him.

But if that were the case, why hadn't he turned himself in to the members of the task force? If not during the chase itself, then why not later? Why had he come to her? Why tell her to keep his presence a secret?

Damn you, she thought as she stared down at him,

trying to figure out if that scenario really made sense, or if she just wanted it to. Her hypothesis did fit the evidence, she decided, but the same evidence would also support the reverse, namely that he'd faked his death so he could drop off the grid entirely and go to work for the terrorists, then got separated from them in the melee of the task force raid on the terrorists' cabin.

Both hypotheses fit, but which was the right one? Or was there yet another explanation she hadn't come up with?

"That doesn't matter right now," she said aloud. "What matters is what you're going to do with him." She glanced at the note, brain spinning.

She knew Romo, knew what he'd been through as a child, and how those experiences had shaped the man he'd become. That, more than anything, told her logic favored the undercover theory. The Romo she'd known had been all about justice, sometimes to the exclusion of all other, softer emotions. She had to believe he'd been working for the good guys. That didn't explain why he wanted to stay in hiding, but it did suggest that if the wrong people found out he was still alive, he could be in very real danger.

Which, if she followed that line of thought to its conclusion, explained why he'd come to her if he felt he couldn't go to whoever he'd been working for. She'd had her full medical training before deciding to specialize in pathology, and kept a small set of supplies on hand in case of emergencies. He would've known that, would've known she could patch him up. And, damn him, he would've known that she'd be unable to turn him away.

Shaking her head, Sara stared down at him. "You're really a bastard, you know that?"

He didn't answer. Didn't even twitch. Which was so not helpful.

She could call an ambulance, then dragoon one of her trusted cop friends to watch over him. There might be suspicions of complicity within the BCCPD and local FBI field office, but she knew for a fact that Chelsea, Fax, Cassie, Seth, Alyssa and Tucker were among the good guys. There was no way any of them were involved with the terrorists. They'd help keep Romo safe.

But Sara stalled, because he'd come to *her*. He'd asked *her* to keep his presence a secret. Maybe, just maybe, it made the most sense to follow his instructions for the moment, and make her decisions once he was conscious and could fill in some of the blanks.

Warning bells chimed at the back of her brain, but she couldn't deal with them just then. She needed to make a decision, and it had better be the right one. Except when she came down to it, she knew she'd made her decision the moment she stepped toward him rather than away; the moment she'd touched his injured shoulder and felt warm skin, and remembered what they'd once been to each other.

"Fine," she said, her words seeming too loud in the silence of her secluded home. "Have it your way. You always did." Reaching for a double handful of his clothing—and steeling herself to be a doctor rather than a woman who still, inexplicably, wanted to weep—she said, "I need to roll you. This is going to hurt."

She doubted he could hear her. The warning was more for her own sake than his, because she wasn't used to dealing with patients who still had their pain responses intact.

Doing her best to minimize the amount she twisted and moved him, in case the bullet had ended up someplace grim, she levered him partway up and checked for an exit wound or other injuries on the front of his body. She didn't find either, which was both good news and bad: good news because his injury seemed localized and treatable, assuming the bullet hadn't punched through to something internal; bad news because she didn't know where the damned thing had gone.

Easing him back down onto his flat stomach, trying not to remember how he'd slept like that, his face smashed into the pillow, his long limbs sprawled toward her, onto her, some part of him always touching some part of her, she rose and headed deeper into the house, through the smallish, oddly arranged rooms that she'd decorated to blend one into the next, with neutral, mossy colors and richly patterned curtains.

She took the stairs leading up to her office and the bedroom, and tried not to remember the night she and Romo had made love on the landing, early in their relationship. They'd been out with her friends, teasing each other with looks and touches, with no question in either of their minds where and how the night would end. They hadn't even made it all the way up the stairs before they'd collapsed, twined together, needing each other so much it had seemed like madness.

Blushing, she stepped into her office, crossing

quickly to the locked gun cabinet in the far corner, where she kept not only the small .22-caliber handgun she'd purchased just after al-Jihad's reign of terror began, but also her medical supplies. The elegant cabinet was far more graceful—and much less expensive— than a safe. She dialed in the combination and popped the door, then stood and stared for a second at the large tackle box she'd outfitted as a field kit.

She'd freshened her supplies regularly over the past year. With al-Jihad hitting targets in and around Bear Claw, she'd wanted to be prepared for emergencies. She'd never actually used the thing, though. Had hoped she'd never have to. She couldn't handle the immediacy of living medicine, the emotions. Now, facing the prospect of working on a man she'd known intimately, a man she'd loved, she quailed. She'd never understood how her mother reveled in the godlike act of cutting into living flesh. Then again, she'd failed to understand a number of her mother's choices over the years.

You can do this, she told herself, squaring her shoulders and reaching for the medical kit. *You* have *to do this.* He'd trusted her enough to put his life and safety in her hands. She would reward that trust by patching him up. *Then, once he's awake, I'll get some answers out of him,* she thought as she returned to his side. Now that she had a plan of sorts, her emotions were starting to shift from dizzying relief at finding him incredibly, impossibly alive…to anger at the deception he'd perpetrated, and his presumption that she'd take him in and treat his wounds on the basis of a note that explained less than nothing.

Leave it to slick, handsome, charming Romo Sampson to assume she'd take care of him after what he'd done to her.

"Bastard," she muttered under her breath, holding on to the anger because it steadied her hands as she cut away his jacket and black T-shirt, revealing the strong lines of his back, the angry bullet wound and the streaks of forming bruises.

She removed the bulk of his clothing, save for his boxers, which were cheap chain-store wear, and nothing like what he would've worn before.

Shoving that thought aside, she piled several blankets over him, then turned up the heat in the living room. She had to get him warm and find a way to get his fluid volume up. But at the same time, she knew she had to be smart, too; she needed to protect herself if things proved more complicated than her more optimistic hypothesis—that he'd been undercover, the blood spatter was from a clean kill of one of the terrorists, and he was in the clear, fully sanctioned for whatever he'd done.

A quiver in her belly warned that the explanation, when she got it, probably wouldn't be that neat. Romo had never been one to make things easy—either on her or on himself.

His clothes were damp with sweat and blood, and streaked with dirt and other substances. His pockets were empty save for her spare key; a quick search revealed that he wasn't carrying any wallet, ID, or weapon. She placed his clothes and boots in a paper bag and taped it shut, signing her name across the tape. Then she locked the bag in the gun cabinet. It wasn't a perfect chain of evidence and probably wouldn't be admissible in court, but it was the best she could do under the circumstances.

It's just in case, she told herself, and worked very hard not to think about what some of those cases might be.

Returning to him, she found that his color was a little better, his flesh a little warmer beneath the blankets. It seemed very strange that her patient's skin was flesh-toned and body temperature, but she shoved aside the oddity, locking it down along with her emotions and telling herself to woman up and do what needed doing.

She set him up on a portable monitor that told her what she already knew: his blood pressure, pulse and respiration were all dangerously depressed. Knowing she needed to get his vitals headed on the upswing, she started him on a saline drip. If it came to it, she'd transfuse him with her own blood. She was a type O, a universal donor. But God help her, she hoped it didn't come to that. She'd already given him everything she intended to of her inner self.

Soon, though, his numbers started coming back up, and his skin and gums pinked, indicating that the shock was fading. Which left her with the bullet wound.

She followed the bruise tracks with her fingers, probing as deeply as she dared. She found three spots where she was pretty sure she felt something. The bullet had fragmented. Damn it.

Doing the best she could, she pulled on sterile gloves, cleaned and numbed the three spots, then chose one and used a scalpel to dissect away the skin and muscle. Without clamps or suction, blood welled immediately, obscuring her working field. She cursed and blotted it with a sterile pad, but gave that up almost immediately as pointless. Instead, she resigned herself to working blind, probing with the scalpel, then forceps.

"Come on…come on…" She was breathing heavily, sweating more from nerves than exertion. Then she felt the forceps lock on to something hard and metallic. "Ah! Gotcha."

She dropped the bloodstained fragment in a specimen jar, used stitches to close the muscle and incision and then repeated the process twice more. By the time she was done, she'd nearly gotten used to the fact that when she cut into him, he bled. Yet although his vitals had stabilized where they needed to be, he hadn't moved or made a sound. He just lay there, breathing. In and out. In and out.

Forcing herself not to watch the rhythmical fall of his back, she returned to her work, stitching up the last of the three cuts before turning her attention to the recovered fragments. When she pieced the ragged bits of metal together in their specimen jar, it looked as though she'd gotten all of the projectile. The metal was deformed, making it impossible for her to be sure, but without an X-ray, there wasn't much more she could do.

She cleaned the entry wound as best she could, then closed it as well, leaving a spot at the bottom for drainage. Finally, she hit her patient with a whopping dose of a broad-spectrum antibiotic. That, plus crossing her fingers, was going to have to be enough. She debated over the painkiller choices she had on-hand, and went with the mildest. He'd be hurting when he awoke—she deliberately thought "when," not "if," as though positive thinking would be enough to pull him out of the deep unconsciousness that continued to hold on to him. But it was that very unconsciousness that meant she couldn't give him one of the stronger painkillers, which had sedative effects.

She needed him to wake up, needed to get a grip on whether the head injury that had blown his pupils to uneven sizes had caused serious damage. If it had, she'd be doing him a major injustice keeping him hidden. But it wasn't as if she had a CAT scan or an MRI handy.

Her training warred with her conscience. She knew she should take him to the ER, where he could be properly cared for. But at the same time, despite what had happened between them, she had to believe that Romo never would have perpetuated a fraud of any sort—never mind faking his own death—if it hadn't been absolutely necessary.

As a child, he'd lived through scandal and a trial when his businessman father had been framed for embezzlement by a coworker. Thanks to solid police work and an ambitious public defender on her way up the political ladder, Romo's father had been acquitted, the other man jailed. Gratitude, and that early exposure to justice, had set Romo on his path to a career in law enforcement.

Sara had heard the story for the first time at his funeral. She also hadn't realized he'd come to Bear Claw via the Las Vegas PD. That it'd taken his funeral for her to learn that much about his past had bothered her. At the same time, it'd made her wish she could have one last chance to confront him. She'd imagined herself demanding to know what had gone wrong between them, why he'd done what he'd done, even knowing about her past and how badly his actions would hurt her.

Now, though, her sketchy knowledge of his childhood only served to reinforce Sara's instinct to follow the instructions in his note. He'd gone into police work looking for justice, undoubtedly moving into internal affairs for the same reason. And though he might leave something to be desired on a personal level, she simply couldn't see him joining the terrorists' cause.

Having done what she could for him, she leaned back on her heels and considered her options. She couldn't lift him by herself, and even if she could, she'd risk tearing the heck out of the stitches. So he'd be staying on the floor for the time being. She did manage, through a combination of leverage and no small amount of tugging, to get a thin camping mattress underneath him, helping keep him warm as well as getting him off the bloodstained floor.

"I'll deal with the cleanup later," she said aloud, wrinkling her nose. But, the immediate issues dealt with, she became aware that she was a mess, and the room didn't smell all that pretty. Maybe she should deal with cleanup sooner than later. This was her home, after all.

Trying not to wonder why he'd come to her rather than whoever he'd been working with since his faked death, she moved around the house, closing the curtains and shutting the blinds, lest a casual—or not so casual—

observer chanced to look in the windows. As she did so, small shivers marched their way along her skin, warning her that she hadn't yet thought through all the ramifications of what she'd done, or the question of what she was planning to do next.

Life or death, he'd written. If the terrorists knew about him, if he feared they would kill him if he surfaced, then wouldn't it stand to reason that they'd be looking for him? But if that were the case, why wouldn't he want Fax, Seth and the few other agents he trusted to know he was alive? Again, why had he come to her?

That made her pause. What if he really *had* been working for—

"No," she said aloud, refusing to go there. The Romo she'd known would never in a million years have switched sides. She knew that for certain. Everything else was just going to have to wait until he woke up.

Still, partly because she didn't want him hurting himself if he started thrashing, partly because her head wasn't quite as sure of him as her heart wanted to be, she pulled a couple of bungee cords from the camping equipment she kept piled in her office closet. Wrapping the cords around his waist and over his wrists, she bound his arms, then did the same with his ankles.

He didn't stir over the next couple of hours, as she showered and changed, made herself a quick dinner and then freshened the living room as best she could. Finally, near midnight, her body drained of the frenetic, nervous energy that had been driving her up to that point, and she sagged with a sudden onslaught of fatigue.

Romo was stable enough for her to detach the monitors and saline as he moved into the recovery phase of his injuries, when she'd need to be watching for infection or other signs that she'd missed something with the relatively crude care she'd been able to provide. Telling herself it only made sense to stay near him, in case problems arose during the night, she clicked on a nightlight in the kitchen to provide a low level of illumination, and bedded down on the couch with a couple of pillows and a thick, soft afghan.

Although she ached with fatigue, her brain kept her restless and wide-awake for far too long. It took almost superhuman effort not to watch him sleep and wonder what had happened to him, what would happen next. It was even harder to keep herself from remembering their times together, both good and bad, all of them tainted with the ache of betrayal and heartache. Eventually, though, she dozed. As she did, she let her hand dangle off the edge of the couch, so her fingertips just brushed the edges of his blanket. Finally, she slipped into a deep sleep.

She awoke hours later, roused by a sound, or maybe just an instinct. Going into doctor mode, she rolled over and moved to rise, opening her eyes as she did so. She froze for a half second at the sight of the empty spot where Romo had been.

Panic sluiced through her and she moved to react, but it was already too late. A man's figure rose above her, silhouetted in the dim light. She saw the glint of his eyes and teeth, and the shadows of his hands as he reached for her, grabbed on to her, his grip hard and hurtful.

Screaming, she exploded from the couch, but it was

already too late. His hands covered her mouth and pressed her back down into the cushions, cutting off her air. Smothering her.

HE BORE DOWN while his enemy grabbed his hands, his wrists, her fingernails digging in as she fought, squirming and bucking against him. And yes, it was a woman, though that didn't make her any less the enemy. Why else had she kept him bound as she slept? She was one of them. One of the ones who hunted him, who wanted him dead. One of the ones whose faces had haunted him in his nightmares and dragged him back to consciousness.

"Who are you?" he said, his voice rasping with the effort his weakened self was expending to hold on to her, as sharp pain flared in his shoulder.

She whiplashed against him, her legs kicking out and meeting nothing but air. *Not a trained fighter,* his brain cataloged, but he already could've guessed that from the way she'd bound him, with cords that had stretched easily under pressure.

He must've been weaker than he'd thought, though, because seconds later she got away from him, clawing and kicking. She hit the floor hard, scrambled up and bolted for the door, screaming.

"Damn it!" Heart hammering—and not just from the fight—he lunged and his legs folded beneath him. Landing hard, he reached out with his good arm, snagged her by an ankle and yanked, bringing her down with him. Strength failing, head pounding with a relentless beat, he went with expediency and lay full length atop her, pinning her with his weight.

She struggled, still screaming, though her screams had turned to words. A name. *Romo*.

He didn't know the name, not really, but he was starting to remember the room. They had fallen halfway into a kitchen; a small night-light was on, allowing him to see more details of the homey, feminine space, and triggering the memory of coming to the house earlier in the day, knowing he'd be safe.

But if he was safe, why the hell had she tied him up? And why the hell was he practically naked?

Scowling, he glared down at his captive. She'd gone still and had stopped screaming, but her face was pale even in the diffuse light, her eyes stark and staring. And a hell of a face it was, too, even terrified.

He couldn't tell the color of her eyes or hair, beyond knowing that they were both light-hued. But the dimness didn't detract from the elegant lines of her face and swanlike neck, the sculpted arches of her eyebrows and the wide bow of her mouth. Beneath him, her body was lithe and strong—he could feel that strength in the sore places on his shin and arms, and the burn of his injured shoulder where she'd yanked against him in her struggles. But although she was strong, she was also wholly feminine, her curves pressing against him, bringing a stir of memory—this one older and more deeply buried.

As he lay atop her, he belatedly realized that he'd come here, to this woman, because he'd trusted her to help him.

Shame washed through him. Guilt. "I'm sorry," he said, though he didn't let her up. "I was dreaming. Nightmare. Then I woke up, not sure where I was, and my arms and legs were tied."

She took a shallow breath and he thought she might scream again. Instead, she said, "Your note didn't give me much to go on. I was trying not to be stupid. Apparently, the bungees were borderline on the stupid factor." He gave her credit for guts, though even as she tried to play it cool, her voice shook.

A roil of memories he couldn't pin down, couldn't place, had him stilling and loosening his hold, then rolling onto his side, taking her with him. She was free to move away, but she didn't. Instead, she lay there facing him, her eyes searching his.

"Where have you been?" she asked, her voice hitching on a suppressed sob. "What happened to you?"

I don't know. I don't even know who I am. Who you are. Who we were together. That was what he should've said. Instead, he found himself staring, filling himself with the sight of her. Though he was no longer touching her, he felt her curves as though they'd been imprinted on his flesh, creating new memories to replace the ones that were gone. A wellspring of loneliness surged from nowhere and everywhere at once—an ache of longing and a deep sense of loss.

He reached for her blindly, moving purely on instinct. Incredibly, she met him halfway in a kiss that started soft and gentle. Then her lips parted on a small moan of surrender and he slipped his tongue inside to touch hers, tangle with hers. He stroked her hair, her face. She cupped his cheek in her palm.

And, for the first time since he'd regained consciousness in the forest, he felt as though he was exactly where he belonged.

Chapter Four

Sara had seen the kiss coming, and could've pulled away if she'd wanted to. Nothing was holding her in place...except her own memories of the two of them together, and the grief she'd felt standing at his graveside. He'd been dead. Now he was alive.

That was why, when he leaned in, she met his kiss. That was why, when he touched his tongue to hers, she returned the move in kind and crowded closer to him so their bodies aligned, though lightly. And that was why, when her blood and body heated at the feel of his bare skin beneath her fingertips and the taste of him on her tongue, she didn't retreat as she knew she should. Instead, she crowded closer, mindful of his injuries but wanting for a moment—just a brief, beautiful moment— to pretend that the past year or so had been a bad dream.

His taste was sharp with pain and fear, but underneath those flavors was that of the man she'd known, deep and complex, rich and multilayered. Her heart kicked in her chest as she soaked in the sensation of touching him and being touched, cherished his soft groan, and the softening of his caress to one of pleasure, and acceptance.

She let herself linger a moment more, then ended the kiss. Regret pierced her as she drew away from him— or had he pulled away first? She didn't know, knew only that now they were lying on her living room floor facing each other, looking into each other's eyes, and he was there, really there after all these months.

And, she realized with a bite of disquiet, he still had the power to make her forget her better intentions, at least for a while.

Damn him.

Fanning the anger because it was a far safer emotion than any of the others he brought out in her, she sat up and glared at him. "If you tore your stitches, I'm going to leave you leaking." Which wasn't the most important issue by far, but was somehow the first thing that had come out of her mouth.

He just looked up at her for a moment, all hard muscles and man, sharp facial angles and clever dark green eyes, with a layer of masculine stubble on his square jaw and the thick dark hair that she'd delighted touching as they'd kissed, as they'd made love. *No,* she told herself, *don't think about that now, don't remember those times. The present is far more important than the past, under the circumstances.*

But before she could demand an explanation of where he'd been for the past several months, he said, "I'm sorry."

It wasn't clear whether he was apologizing a second

time for grabbing her, for disappearing and faking his own death, for kissing her or for potentially having messed up her stitches. Since she wasn't actually sure which she would've preferred, she let it go, asking instead, "What happened to you?"

"I...I'm not sure." He sat up slowly and started climbing to his feet, dragging one of the blankets with him in the absence of clothing. He was clearly feeling his injuries now that his body was draining of the adrenaline spike that must've powered him to this point.

Sara rose and gripped his good arm when he swayed, even though her own legs were far from steady. Forcing herself to focus on the practical stuff when nothing else seemed to make any sense, she said, "Come on. As long as you're on your feet, let's get you to the bedroom." She had a feeling he'd be headed for a collapse once the last of the adrenaline had burned off, and would rather he didn't wind up on the floor again.

He leaned on her heavily as they climbed the stairs to the second floor. She told herself to ignore the fact that he was mostly naked, that her hands gripped the warm, lithe flesh that had brought her such pleasure in the past. She watched his face as they crossed the spot where they'd made love so long ago. When his expression didn't change, she cursed him for being an insensitive ass, and cursed herself for caring when they'd been broken up for more than a year, and he'd been dead—in theory, anyway—for nearly half that time.

He hesitated at her office door, and she urged him past it to her bedroom, where he lay facedown on the bed with a grateful, pained sigh. He stayed obediently still while she checked his wounds, which were inflamed and angry, but showed little sign of additional damage.

"You got lucky," she said, pulling the blanket up over him. "The stitches held." Then, feeling unaccountably jittery, she sat on the edge of the bed they used to share, spinning to face him and perch there, crosslegged. He looked at her, expression unreadable, as she inhaled a deep breath and let it out again in a slow, measured exhale that did little to settle her sudden nerves. "Okay," she said. "Here's the deal. I didn't call an ambulance or the cops, and I didn't tell anyone you were here because of your note, and because we have enough of a history for me to give you the benefit of the doubt. But also considering our history, I think you'll agree that I don't owe you much more than that. So if you want me to keep helping you out, you're going to have to give me a reason and some explanations, starting now."

Although he was lying in her bed, injured and lacking the strength to stand on his own, his expression was intense as he reached out to her with his good hand and gripped her fingers in his. "Thank you for not turning me in."

Something shivered down her spine at his choice of words. "Tell me you're going to call Fax and Seth now, or whoever you've been working for within the PD."

He grimaced. "I'd like to say yes, but…" He trailed off, his expression clouding. After a moment, he said, "Okay, I'm going to tell you the truth because whatever the details, I apparently trust you more than I do anyone else in the area."

She frowned, confused. "I...I don't know what that means."

He tightened his fingers on hers. "It means that I don't know your name. I don't know my own name. I don't know what we were to each other, or why our relationship—judging from what you just said, anyway—ended. And I damn sure don't know who shot me, or why."

Sara felt the blood drain from her face, and imagined she'd just gone very pale. Which was okay, because she had a feeling she was about to faint. "You don't...."

He shook his head. "Not a clue. I've got nothing. Why don't you tell me what you know about what I've been up to lately, and we'll see if anything jogs a memory."

A bubble of near-hysterical laughter pressed on Sara's windpipe. "You...you don't remember any of it?"

He turned one hand palm-up. "Obviously I remember the walking-around skills, like how to drive, and that it was a damn good idea to cover up with the jacket so nobody would see my back. But that's survival stuff. I don't—" He broke off, throat working. "I don't remember the things that make me an individual." He tried for a grin. "The only thing I know is that I've got good taste in beautiful, capable women who deal well in a crisis."

"Good taste, maybe, but also a roving eye," she said quellingly, trying not to let him see how much the words cost her. "But that was more than a year ago. In the interim, you died in a prison riot. I watched your parents bury you."

Whatever he'd been about to say in regards to his

fidelity—or lack thereof—died on his lips, and his face went blank with shock. "You're kidding."

"That's so not something I would kid about."

"Why in the hell would I fake my own death?"

Sara hesitated, trying to sublimate her own swirling emotions to the practicalities demanded by the situation. As a doctor, she knew she should let him rest. Retrograde amnesia, whether from a head injury or mental trauma—or both—could pass quickly…or it could prove permanent. If she bided her time, the memories might start coming back on their own, with less shock than she was likely to cause by telling him about the terrorists, the prison riot and his own disappearance. Unfortunately, she didn't think she had the luxury of time to let him remember on his own. The amnesia fit into her theory that he'd been undercover, explaining why he hadn't gone to whoever had been overseeing the operation. But it also fit into the less-likely-seeming possibility that he'd been with the terrorists voluntarily, then run from them during the chaos of the manhunt. He hadn't known which side he was working for, or even what was going on.

In either case, she realized, the terrorists and cops would both be looking for him. And she couldn't do the logical thing and turn him in to the task force, because al-Jihad's people had infiltrated the official response at almost every level. Until they knew who Romo had been reporting to, and whether he trusted that contact, keeping him hidden could truly be a life-or-death scenario, as his note had said.

She had to tell him about the situation, she decided,

and hope the information would help him remember who he could trust. But that left the question of where to begin the story.

As if reading the question in her face, he said softly, "Start with the two of us. Why did I come here?"

That was easy. "We were lovers. You even lived here for a few months before we broke up. That was about a year ago."

"You said I had a roving eye," he said. "I was unfaithful?"

"Once." Which had been enough for her. She'd made a point never to give second chances in situations like that. She wasn't her mother. "It was a long time ago, though, and not really pertinent to what's going on."

Rather than dragging him through a one-sided post-mortem of their yearlong love affair, she told him about how al-Jihad, Lee Mawadi and Muhammad Feyd had orchestrated simultaneous bombings in shopping malls across Colorado just prior to Christmas several years earlier, killing hundreds, including a large number of children who'd been waiting to see the mall Santas.

She described how, after a lengthy trial during which Lee Mawadi's ex-wife, Mariah, was briefly suspected of complicity and then exonerated, the three powerful terrorists were convicted for the Santa Bombings and sent to the ARX Supermax Prison north of Bear Claw City. There, through the sort of clandestine communication network that tended to exist in supermax security prisons despite the inmates' isolation, al-Jihad made contact with Jonah Fairfax, who was supposedly doing life without parole for killing two federal agents during a raid on an antigovernment cult up in Montana. In reality, he was a deep undercover operative tasked with ferreting out al-Jihad's contacts within federal law enforcement. In that guise, his handler encouraged him to help al-Jihad and his lieutenants escape. That same handler, Jane Doe, had been working with the terrorists all along. Fax had turned out to truly be one of the good guys, despite Sara's concerns when her best friend, Chelsea, had fallen for the escaped-convict-maybe-undercover-agent. He and Chelsea's friends had banded together to foil a terror attack on a local concert, recapturing Muhammad Feyd in the process. The others—including Jane Doe—had remained at large, though, and intelligence suggested they had fled the country.

A few months later, Lee Mawadi had reappeared in the Bear Claw area, gunning for his ex-wife, Mariah. Sara was less clear on the details, except to say that the ex was now engaged to one of the FBI agents on the task force. The two had been instrumental in foiling a planned attack on the prison, though they hadn't stopped the riot that had killed—supposedly, anyway—Detective Romo Sampson of the BCCPD's internal affairs department. Who patently wasn't dead.

Finishing up, Sara told him how over the past few weeks the communication monitors had said things were heating up the way they might before another attack. Nobody knew where the next horror would be targeted, though, or when. She paused. "There was a manhunt today. Two federal agents were killed, maybe a couple of the terrorists, too…and then you show up here covered in blood."

His eyes were very dark, though she couldn't read the emotions in them. "I don't know whose blood it was," he grated. "God help me, but I don't know. I don't even know whose side I'm on."

"You're one of the good guys," she said automatically. "You must've been undercover, working for al-Jihad and his people, while reporting back to someone on the local or federal response team."

"You sound very sure of that, considering our history." He paused. "What exactly happened between us?"

Unease was a sluice of cold in her belly. "You sure you want to go there?"

"Yeah." His smile went crooked. "I can't imagine…I don't feel like the kind of guy who would cheat."

Her heart drummed in her chest, with a relentless, aching beat. "Trust me, you did. Then you came to me the next morning and confessed. You said you'd stopped into a bar, had a few, one thing led to another…and you woke up next to your waitress."

He winced, but struggled to lever himself up on an elbow, even though the action must've hurt like fury. His eyes were steady on hers, his gaze deep and probing, making her very aware of his bare collarbones and throat, and the fact that he was all but naked beneath the blanket. "Did I ask you for another chance?"

Her face felt numb, her whole body felt numb. She couldn't believe she was having this conversation with a dead man who didn't even know his own name. "I don't do second chances."

Something flickered in his expression. "Pity. That was a hell of a kiss."

She squared her shoulders as anger guttered. "We were great in bed. In the end, that wasn't enough." He looked as though he wanted to say something more, but she steamrolled over him, snapping, "And is that the only thing you can think about, after what I just told you?"

"Of course not. But it's the elephant in the room, isn't it?"

He was right, of course. They weren't strangers, but in a sense they were, because he didn't remember the things she did—assuming she could believe him about the amnesia. She did believe him, though, because no matter how many times she'd called him a cheat and a liar inside her own head, the truth was that he'd never lied. He'd told her about the waitress the next morning. If he hadn't lied about that, she couldn't believe he was lying now. Which left them—where?

She shook her head, not sure what came next. "You should get some sleep, let some of this gel."

"Actually, what I should do is leave," he said bluntly. "I shouldn't have come here. I just… It was instinct."

The fact that she found that even the slightest bit flattering just went to show how thoroughly she'd been into him. And also that she was her mother's daughter.

"If you leave, I doubt you'll get far," she said dryly.

His eyes went to the window, even though she'd drawn the curtain earlier, blocking out the night. "You're probably right. I've endangered you by coming here. Whether I leave or not, you'll still be a target."

A chill swept over her. "I was talking about the fact that I doubt you'd make it far without collapsing, given the concussion, bullet wound and blood loss." But he was right about the other, too, she knew. People were looking for him. Regardless of who found him first, she was going to be in serious trouble. If the task force found out she'd hidden him, Percy would have his excuse to fire her. If the terrorists found him, they were both dead.

She should turn him in, to Fax or someone she trusted. But what if the blood on his clothing had come from the dead agents? Even Fax was on a witch hunt to cull all the conspirators from the federal ranks, and none of her friends had thought much of Romo in the wake of the breakup. Could she truly trust them to believe in him the way she did?

Damn it, she didn't know what to do, and she hated not knowing what came next. She'd grown up in a family that had been in a constant state of flux, with her father coming and going depending on where her parents had been in the cycle of him cheating, her kicking him out, him repenting and her forgiving him. Over and over again.

"You're a doctor?" Romo asked, no doubt because she'd just predicted he'd fall on his face if he tried to leave now.

"I'm—" She broke off, struck anew by just how odd it was for him to be meeting her for the first time all over again, after they'd been as intimate as two people could possibly be. Or at least as intimate as he'd let them be. "I'm the chief ME of Bear Claw City," she said, and even she heard the quiet ring of pride in the words. And why not? The job might not be hers for much longer, but for now she could claim the prestigious title.

He whistled. "Impressive." He frowned for a moment, thinking.

"What?"

"Nothing." He shook his head. "It's just that it's true, you know. You're in danger now because I came here."

"I have friends who could help."

Romo's expression went instantly shuttered. "Don't tell any of them that I'm here. Don't even hint it. Promise me."

His sudden intensity sent a spear of worry through her. "Why not?"

"I don't want to endanger them the same way I've endangered you," he said, but she had a feeling there was more to it than that.

"They're all cops and agents, Romo. They can handle themselves." She wasn't as sure as she sounded, though. The memory of his funeral was too close to the surface. She couldn't bear to think of reliving the experience for Chelsea, Fax or any of the others.

"Promise me," he repeated, reaching out as though he wanted to touch her, though they were a room apart. "Promise you'll give me the night to remember. Promise me we'll talk again before you do anything."

They stared at each other for a long moment while the air thickened with things said and unsaid, and with too many questions. Finally, unable to deal with the pressure that gathered in her chest and made her want impossible things, she turned away. "Get some rest.

I'm going to call Tucker. He's a homicide detective with the BCCPD. If I tell him the manhunt has me freaked out, he'll send a patrol past here every hour or so." It didn't seem like nearly enough, but it was all she could think to do just then. She couldn't leave her patient, couldn't move him, couldn't kick him out... and she'd just promised not to turn him in until at least morning.

"And one other thing."

"What?" she asked, but the word came out weakly, as exhaustion rushed over her, swamping her. Her brain was full, her heart heavy. She just wanted to shut it all off for a little while.

"You called me Romo."

She stilled, her heart cracking a little, bleeding for what he'd lost, for the uncertainty of when—or even if—he'd get it all back. "That's your name. Detective Romo Sampson, Internal Affairs, Bear Claw Creek."

"And you?"

"Sara Whitney."

He said her name back to himself. "Pretty name."

The offhand comment shouldn't have touched her as deeply as it did. Because of that, because of the weakness it indicated, she backed out the door. "I'm going now. Sleep. And don't stress your stitches."

She closed the door firmly at her back, not to keep him in, but to remind herself to keep out. Romo wasn't hers anymore. He hadn't been for a long, long time.

AS THE DOOR SHUT, he lay still, staring after her, trying on his own name. *Romo Sampson.* It was a good enough handle, he supposed, ignoring the lick of panic that came when he realized he didn't know what "Romo" was short for, if anything. He didn't remember the name, didn't remember the parents who'd given it to him, or the woman he'd instinctively come to for help.

An ex-girlfriend, he thought, trying to align that information with his almost overwhelming desire to roll across the big bed with her, and do something to blunt the roiling, churning lust that had gripped him low in the gut the moment he'd pressed his body against hers, the moment he'd kissed her.

Mine, his entire being had said at that moment. And she had cooperated fully, making it something of a shock to learn that they weren't together, hadn't been for some time. Somewhere in his banged-up head, he'd been sure they were a couple. Apparently, he'd forgotten their breakup. He'd forgotten a whole lot of things, and he had a feeling lots of what he'd forgotten wasn't at all pleasant.

Sara seemed convinced he'd been undercover. He wasn't so sure. But as he lay there, trying to remember something—anything—the gray-brown crept in on the edges of his vision, taking over everything. Willing or not, he slept.

Hours later, he awoke stiff and sore, with an excessively foul taste in his mouth. A dim light shone from the bathroom, and when he made it in there, he found a couple of pain pills and a glass for tap water. He downed the pills and water, and stood there, braced against the sink with his head hanging and his shoulder on fire.

He should go back to bed and give his body more healing time, he knew, but his half-remembered dreams kept him on his feet.

His head throbbed, tangling the present with occasional flashes of what he could only assume were things from his past. They weren't in any sort of order, though, didn't have any context. He hoped to hell the flashes themselves were evidence that his memory would come back quickly, as whatever swelling he had going on inside his skull came back down to a dull roar. Problem was, a part of him wasn't sure he wanted those memories back—they were starting to show him some seriously grim scenes, ones suggesting he hadn't been quite the nice guy Sara seemed to believe.

He saw blood and heard a man's screams, saw a computer with a set of schematics on it. And he had an overwhelming sense that he needed to be doing something, performing some sort of mission, but he was damned if he knew what he was supposed to be doing.

Panic stirred. He was unarmed, unprotected. And he wasn't sure the thought of the local cops doubling their patrols was much of a comfort; first, because from the sounds of it, the terrorists had been running rings around them for months; and second, because for all he knew, the cops were the ones looking for him.

He should leave, he knew. Unfortunately, he was realistic enough to admit that he wouldn't get far. He was too damned weak to run. What was more, he'd been there too long already. Whoever was looking for him might've found him already. If so, he couldn't very well leave Sara, knowing she was in danger. He owed her better than running away. He owed her protection, through the morning, at least.

Pushing away from the sink, he headed for the bedroom door, remembering that he'd glimpsed a gun cabinet in the office next door to the bedroom. Almost as an afterthought, he realized he was wearing cheapo skivvies and nothing else. Detouring to her wardrobe, he unearthed a pair of navy blue drawstring sweatpants and a plain black T-shirt that probably swam on Sara's slender frame, but fit snugly across his chest.

The clothing was soft and smelled of her, of laundry detergent and springtime, though he couldn't help noticing the faint odor of blood that came from his own skin, tainting the moment.

Once he was dressed, he slipped out of the bedroom and down the hall to Sara's office. He crossed to the gun cabinet, alert for any noise from the first floor, assuming she'd bunked down on the couch. The gun cabinet was unlocked, which had him muttering about her lack of security. When he got the cabinet open, though, and saw that it was most of the way full with first aid supplies that looked hastily rifled, he figured that explained it. She'd left the cabinet unlocked in her haste to deal with his injuries.

Either that, or there was no gun in there, just medical supplies.

For a moment he thought he was out of luck. Then he caught sight of a small handgun on the top shelf, shoved most of the way to the back next to a box of ammo. Gritting his teeth against a bit of pain, he dug the weapon out and loaded the little .22. Once he had it tucked into his waistband, he felt far better about the situation, and his ability to deal with anyone who tracked him to pretty Sara Whitney's home.

Granted, a .22 wasn't much in the way of firepower, but it was something.

He was about to close up the cabinet when he spied a crumpled paper bag that looked completely out of place amid the sterile first aid supplies. Beside it were his boots. A quick recon showed that the bag held what he suspected were his clothes, packaged as if for evidence. He left the bag alone, but took the boots, carrying them rather than putting him on because he didn't want to wake Sara as he descended the stairs.

Halfway down, on a small, carpeted landing, he paused as a touch of heat feathered across his skin, accompanied by a flare of longing. He grabbed for the memory but it refused to come clear, leaving him feeling hollow. Lonely.

"She's your ex-girlfriend," he reminded himself. "*Ex.* And you're sure as hell not in a position to be thinking about changing her mind on that one." He'd endangered her by his presence. He wouldn't compound that by trying to seduce her.

He wasn't clear on what had happened between them. He didn't think he was the kind of man who cheated; he'd felt a deeply rooted twist of guilt and self-loathing when she'd mentioned it, along with something else that made him think things had been far from simple between them. But complicated or not, he'd reacted to her. And, injured or not, he wanted her.

Still, though, she'd been very clear: no second

chances. And although he didn't know her well—at least not in this incarnation of himself—he had a feeling she didn't make statements like that lightly.

But while logic and rationality said he should leave her alone, when he reached the first floor and found her lying asleep on the sofa where she'd been before— where she'd been when he grabbed her, kissed her—he had to damp down the almost irresistible urge to cross to her, go down on his knees beside the couch and pick up where they'd broken off earlier, with her hands on his face, his buried in her thick, honey-colored hair. That part had been easy, natural. The rest of it, though, was anything but.

Knowing it, and knowing he couldn't live with himself—whoever he was—if anything happened to her, he snagged the bedding he'd been lying on earlier, and cobbled together a makeshift pallet near the front door. It wasn't particularly comfortable, he found as he lay down and felt his bruises howl, his stitches tug. But that had been his plan—the discomfort would keep him from sleeping too deeply despite his injuries, meaning he'd have a better chance of hearing an intruder and responding in time. He hoped.

He lay facing the door for maybe five minutes before he gave in to the temptation and levered himself painfully to his other side, so he could watch Sara sleep. She'd left on the same kitchen night-light as before, and the dim illumination cast soft shadows on her hands, which were tucked beneath her cheek. The pose might have been angelic, but even in repose her face lacked the pure sweetness generally associated with cherubs and angels. No, she exuded an earthy sensuality in the tilt of her high, elegant brows and the purse of her full lips. And there was an energy about her, a sense that she was never quite still, even in sleep, never quite at peace with herself, or maybe with what was going on around her.

Can you blame her? he thought sardonically, because of course he couldn't blame her one bit. But he could, and would, do his best to see that she didn't suffer because she'd helped him.

Forcing himself to turn away, he once again faced the doorway, and shifted the handgun to beneath his pillow, where he could grab it easily if he heard a suspicious noise. Then, knowing he'd better doze and give his body the time and resources to heal, he closed his eyes and put himself into a light, restorative trance he didn't know he knew how to do until after he'd done it.

In the trance he saw sounds as colors, a rainbow of soft nighttime noises, none of which alarmed him. Sinking a level deeper into the self-hypnosis, he heard the same whisper that had been nagging at him since he'd regained consciousness out in the woods. *The mission. Must complete the mission.*

Now, though, that wasn't the only thing he had to do. The mission—whatever the hell it was—might be his priority, but alongside it was another need, one very close to his heart. He had to make sure that Sara didn't suffer for his sins.

Chapter Five

The next morning Sara awoke stiff and sore, and for a moment didn't know where she was. Her living room came clear around her first, reassuring in its familiarity, and she had a half second of thinking she'd fallen asleep in front of the TV, which although rare, was something she did from time to time.

Then she saw the silhouette of a man standing at one of the front windows, peering between the drawn curtains. Heat shimmered through her alongside dread, though it seemed odd that the two could coexist. "See anything?" she asked softly.

His shoulders tensed, but he kept up his surveillance for a moment longer before he turned to her. "An unmarked sedan has been by a couple of times, no doubt thanks to your friend. I haven't seen anything I would consider suspicious."

Sara frowned and sat up on the sofa, rubbing her face to clear the sleep from her system. "How long have you been standing there? You're supposed to be resting that shoulder."

"I can rest when I'm dead for real." He paused. "I borrowed your gun. If that's a problem for you, just say the word and I'll hand it over."

She couldn't see his expression or read his mood, could only see the outline of his body against the light coming through the curtained window. Oddly, though, she wasn't bothered by the thought that he was armed. He'd been a cop when they met, so she was used to him wearing a gun. "Keep it. I'm not the world's best shot." She rose and crossed to him, putting herself between him and the window so she could see his face. "How are you feeling? And don't lie."

"Sore," he admitted. "But alive, thanks to you."

His face was drawn and tired, more gaunt than she remembered, and covered with a day's worth of stubble. She'd never seen him looking so rough before…and she'd never had a stronger impulse to throw herself against him and sob into his chest. Or kiss him. Or pound her fists against him.

Emotions jammed her throat, forcing her to swallow around a huge lump of tears, anger and elation.

His expression changed, going from guarded wariness to concern. "Hey." He reached out to her. "It's okay."

She jolted away, batting at his hands. "It is *not* okay." Part of her wondered if it would ever be okay again. She'd thought she'd gotten used to him being out of her life, first as an ex, then as a dead man. But now, having him standing in front of her…she didn't know how to cope, didn't know if she could.

She'd come to Bear Claw hoping for a calm, orderly

life, one where she could do good work for the ME's office and the young, progressive mayor. She'd found a home and friends she loved, and for a while, a man, as well. Even when her and Romo's relationship had ended, she'd managed to keep things on a relatively even keel, at least outwardly. She'd functioned. She'd dealt. She'd mourned his death. And time had gone on. Except that now, more than a year later, the city was under a terrible threat of violence, her job was on the brink, Romo was back and things were rapidly spinning out of her control.

"We should sit," Romo said. "We need to talk." He took her arm and urged her away from the window, in the direction of the kitchen. "Come on, I'll make us some coffee."

Near-hysterical laughter bubbled up in her chest. "My coffeemaker's busted. I broke it yesterday morning, back when my biggest problems were my wonky windshield wipers, my sticky office door and the acting mayor's vendetta against my staff." But she let him guide her to one of the stools at the breakfast bar. When he started boiling water for tea, finding the bags in the third cabinet he tried, she scrubbed her hands over her face again, and sighed. "God. I hate feeling so out of control."

"Finally. Something we have in common besides what I have to believe was some really great sex."

His offhand comment was so dry, delivered so perfectly, that she laughed in spite of herself. Then again, he'd always had a knack for turning her knee-jerks back on themselves, making her see them for the old patterns they were. That was why she'd agreed to go out with him in the first place, after resisting for nearly a month—he'd convinced her that despite his reputation, he was no playboy. He'd claimed that while he'd dated around when he'd first arrived in Bear Claw, he'd been a serial monogamist, and that a handsome, charismatic devil like himself was no more likely to cheat than any other man, comparisons to her father notwithstanding.

And he'd been right. For a while, anyway.

The memory didn't sour her mood so much as it reminded her of what she'd begun to process the night before, as she'd slid toward sleep—namely that the fact of Romo being alive didn't rewind the months prior to his death. If his funeral hadn't taken away the sins of his life, then neither did his resurrection.

"Here." He deposited a steaming mug of tea on the breakfast bar, took one for himself and made a vague gesture. "You want milk or sugar? Lemon?"

The question was a poignant reminder of how much he'd lost. The old Romo had kept a running file of her likes and dislikes in his head, which she'd taken as evidence that he'd paid attention, that he'd cared. And maybe he'd done both of those things. But he'd also played her.

She shook her head. "This is fine. I take it that means you didn't wake up with all your memories back?"

"I wish." He took the other bar stool, spinning it to face her and covering the wince when the move jarred his injured shoulder.

"You shouldn't be out of bed," she said automatically, though he looked far stronger than she would've expected, given what he'd been through the previous day, and far better than he ought to, wearing her sweats and tee.

"I shouldn't be here," he countered, seeming to search her eyes for a response she wasn't sure she could give.

"If we assume you were working against the terror-ists—and, having known you as well as I did, I'm sticking with that assumption until given reason to doubt it—then I'm probably safer if you stay," she said bluntly. "They'll be looking for you, and eventually they'll look here, based on our past relationship if nothing else. I'd rather not be alone when that happens."

His face darkened. "You should go into protective custody."

"And tell them what?" she countered. "I can lean on Tucker for some extra drive-bys without too much of an explanation, but I'd need more than that to get myself locked down. I'd have to tell them about you, and with-out knowing who you were working for—and therefore who I could trust—I wouldn't be able to control the in-formation flow within the task force. You'd have the cops and al-Jihad after you, doubling the complications you're going to have while you try to remember what you were doing, and for who." She paused and said dryly, "Not to mention that while you're putting on a good show right now, ten bucks says you're fast asleep within the next half hour."

Now that they were in the brightly lit kitchen and the caffeine was kicking in, she could clearly see the grayish cast to his haggard skin, the pain lines beside his mouth and the tired way he favored his injured shoulder and neck.

He grimaced. "Sounds like you've been doing some thinking."

"Hard not to."

"Yeah." He sat for a moment, pensive. "I hate that I've put you in this position. I wish…I don't know. I wish I'd gone any place but here."

"If you had, you'd probably be dead by now," she said with little conceit. "If you'd wound up in the medical system, they would've reported the gunshot injury and whoever is looking for you would've found you. If you holed up somewhere without treatment, you would've died from the shock and blood loss. And although there've been days I would've said I hated you, I'd still much rather have you in this world than not."

That earned her a sharp look, but he said only, "I saw the bag in the gun safe."

At first she winced, thinking he'd take that as a sign of disloyalty. Then she decided that she didn't care if he did. She said, "If you can't remember anything, maybe the evidence can help tell us."

He nodded, expression guarded. "My thoughts exactly. Did you keep the bullet?"

"Yep. I couldn't tell you what caliber it was, though. It fragmented, and is fairly deformed. I'd like to give it to Cassie, along with the clothes." When he stiffened, she said, "Cassie's the top forensic analyst in the BCCPD, and she's a good friend. I trust her with my life."

Do you trust her with mine? Romo's sardonic expression seemed to say. But aloud he said only, "Can you give her the evidence without telling her where it came from?"

"If I told her what was going on, she'd keep it to herself."

He must've seen something in her eyes, though, because he said, "You're not sure of that. You don't trust her."

"I do," she knee-jerked, but then clarified, "It's her husband, Seth. He's one of the top forensic analysts for the FBI, and I can't swear she wouldn't tell him."

"And you don't trust him."

"I trust him to do what he thinks is right, but that's not always what the person in question has asked him to do," she said, remembering a couple of times over the past year that Seth had gone against his word in making his own judgment call. Granted, those instances had worked out for the best, but she wasn't sure she dared run the risk.

Romo shifted in his seat, and was less able to hide the wince this time. "Then either you can't use Cassie for this, or you have to lie to her about where the samples came from. Can you do that?"

The answer should've been a categorical "no." But Sara found herself hesitating. "How about talking to Fax? He was undercover. If anyone knows who you'd be likely to report to, it'd be him."

"That's still assuming I was undercover," Romo said. "What if I wasn't?"

"Then I should definitely turn you in to Fax." She

paused, a little skitter of nerves dancing down her spine. "You're not saying…"

"I don't know what the hell I'm saying anymore. I don't think I'm a bad guy, but how do I know for sure? And if I *was* doing something wrong, then I need to make it right somehow, which means staying free long enough to figure it out." He reached out with his good arm and took one of her hands in his. "I hate that I've put you in this position."

"I'm not too thrilled about it, either." But the strange thing was, she wasn't entirely unhappy about how things were turning out. Surprising them both, she said, "I'll take the samples to Cassie and tell her they came from an informant." It wouldn't exactly be a lie that way.

He looked at her with wary hope. "You'd be willing to do that? Willing to get involved that way?"

She hesitated for a moment before she said, "Normally, the answer would be no. I'm not a risk taker, I like my life simple and this is pretty much the definition of risky and complicated. If I get caught, the acting mayor will fire me in a heartbeat, my friends will know I lied to them and I'll probably face some major charges. Not to mention what might happen to you. But the thing is, Bear Claw is my home, and it's under siege. If I can do something to help fix that, then I guess I have to, don't I?" Those were only some of the conclusions she'd come to as she'd dozed off, decisions that had been cemented in her mind as she'd slept.

Hiding from the police reports and task force bulletins because she'd felt she couldn't do anything to help was one thing. Refusing to do something that actually *might* help was another. And besides, regardless of how things had ended between her and Romo, the history was there. She couldn't turn him in until she was sure of his guilt. She just couldn't.

He squeezed her hand. "You're a brave woman."

"I never was before," she answered. "Maybe now is the time to start."

By midmorning, though, she wasn't feeling at all brave. She just felt like a total sneak.

She had falsified official documentation and basically lied her ass off to get Cassie to fast-track the processing of blood samples from two small pieces cut from Romo's shirt, and the analysis of the bullet fragments he'd had in his back.

Cassie, of course, didn't know that was where they'd come from. Sara had sent them over as "don't ask, don't tell" samples, which in task-force speak pretty much meant what it said. With so much of the suspicion falling within the law enforcement agencies themselves, there were undercover stings running within undercover stings. At least Sara got the feeling there were—she wasn't in the middle of the information flow. Which, she hoped, wouldn't trip Cassie's suspicions too badly, making her wonder why the heck don't-tell materials were coming through the ME's office.

Once the samples were sent off, Sara plowed through three routine cases while Stephen worked on the two dead agents. True to his word, the other ME had come in to work the cases, even though it was Saturday. On one level, Sara was beyond grateful that she didn't have to deal with those particular bodies, especially given her near certainty that Romo had been among the targets of the federal manhunt. On another level, though, she found herself wanting to be alone in the autopsy theater, wished she could turn off the relentlessly cheerful dance music Stephen liked to play while he worked.

As soon as she finished with the third case, she stripped out of her protective gear, cleaned up and escaped to the peace and quiet of her office, not even bothering to be piqued when the door stuck. She had way bigger problems than that. Like a lover returned from the dead, and the very real possibility that the terrorists, or the cops, or both, were looking for him.

Romo had insisted she carry the .22 when she went in to work. She'd agreed because she'd done the necessary paperwork to carry concealed, and was able to get the weapon through the heightened security measures that now surrounded the buildings that housed the BCCPD and ME's office. And maybe it made her feel slightly safer, knowing she had a means of defense. But still, she hated the necessity, and couldn't bear to imagine actually using the weapon on anything but gun range targets.

Hopefully, I won't have to, she thought morosely, then sighed, dug her fingers into her hair and muttered, "I hate this."

"Trouble?" a voice said from the doorway.

Sara looked up quickly, gasping a little at the jolt of surprise. Cassie stood in the doorway, holding an official-looking folder. Tall and blond, with legs that went a mile and pinup-type curves, Cassie was a bomb-

shell who cared little for her own looks, and wore a
don't-mess-with-me attitude that, according to Alyssa,
anyway, had mellowed a fair bit in the years since her
marriage to Seth.

As far as Sara was concerned, if this was Cassie in
mellow mode, she must've been a holy terror before. Sara
loved Cassie as a friend, but was a little intimidated by her
at the same time. Especially now, under the circumstances.

"Hey!" Sara said, her voice cracking a little with the
effort of trying to sound normal. Knowing the BCCPD's
top forensic evidence analyst missed little, she nodded
to the folder, which was of the sort usually used to
transmit results from one division of the task force to
another. "I didn't expect you to hand-deliver."

"A priority is a priority, especially these days,"
Cassie said matter-of-factly. Her words were friendly
enough, but behind them was a hard edge that was pure
business. The members of the task force—and ancillary
members like Sara herself—had all lost acquaintances
in the attacks, most had lost friends. They were committed to doing whatever it took to break al-Jihad's hold
on the region and bring down his terror cells, including
those potentially rooted within the BCCPD and FBI.

Swallowing against a knot of guilt at deceiving a
friend, Sara asked, "Did you find anything interesting?"
She tensed with hope, because "interesting" could mean
the DNA from the blood spatter was a match to
someone other than the dead agents, or that the bullet
traced to a non–PD weapon. "Interesting" could suggest
Romo hadn't killed either of the agents, that she wasn't
being an enormous idiot by keeping his secret.

"Maybe," Cassie said, her eyes narrowing slightly. "And the hand delivery was because your message made it sound urgent. Which leaves me wondering about the source of DNA samples that didn't come from either of the bodies you're not autopsying." Her telling look went to the autopsy theater, where Stephen was hard at work on the dead agents, who hadn't been wearing clothing the same type as the ones Sara had sent over. Cassie looked back at her. "What have you gotten yourself into, Sara?"

Heart thudding as her panic level rose, Sara faked a grimace, and said, "I'm doing a favor for a friend who wants to keep a very low profile, that's all." It wasn't a lie. But it didn't feel good, either.

So turn him in, the logical part of her brain whispered. *Tell Cassie right now. Say, "Romo Sampson showed up at my place yesterday, wounded and covered in blood, alive, with no clue where he's been for the past bunch of months, what he's been doing, or who he's been working for."* Yeah, that was what she should say, she knew.

But she didn't.

Cassie gave her a long look, then shook her head. "I hope you know what you're doing."

Me, too, Sara thought wildly, hoping she wasn't in the process of making the biggest mistake of her life. "Did you get a hit on the DNA?"

Frustration glinted briefly in the analyst's eyes. "No, damn it. No matches in any of the databases. Not even a partial hit off a relative. You've got one male donor, and the DNA is useless until you've got another sample to compare it to."

"Isn't that the story of our lives?" Sara said, and she wasn't faking the regret. Although CODIS grew by leaps and bounds each year, the federal DNA database still only held a fraction of the available samples, and then primarily those belonging to major violent criminals, such as murderers and rapists. Although the repository of DNA profiles held millions of samples, matching an unknown was still a long shot. Cautiously she asked, "Did you check the samples against the PD and military databases?"

Romo would be in them, she knew, and the knowledge strung her tight. She'd been betting the blood contributions from the spatter would overwhelm any sweat contributions from his body, and she'd only given Cassie clothing fragments that hadn't been stained by the blood loss from his shoulder wound, but still, it had been a calculated risk.

Cassie lifted a shoulder. "Military, police. The works. No match."

Sara tried not to let her relief show. "Anything on the bullet or spatter pattern?"

"It's all in here." Cassie lifted the sealed folder.

Sara stopped herself from demanding a summary, reminding herself she was supposed to be nothing more than an educated drop point for some mythical undercover operative. There was no reason for her to want the nitty-gritty, beyond curiosity, and up to this point, she'd made a point of not wanting to know too much about the case, just as she'd tried to avoid the news bulletins the day before.

She'd done her work and helped where she could,

but—especially after Romo's death—had distanced herself from the details. Reversing that now would only draw a level of attention she couldn't afford. Technically, Cassie shouldn't even have done the work she'd asked. But friends trusted friends, which made Sara feel even worse.

"Thanks, I'll pass it along," she said. "Did you want to grab some coffee?" She would've rather kept sulking in her office, but she had a feeling the moment she and Cassie parted company, the astute cop's brain was going to circle back on dangerous questions, and Sara couldn't afford to let that happen. *Romo* couldn't afford for her to let it happen.

Cassie checked the time on her cell, and made a rueful face. "Rain check? I've got a meeting in twenty."

"Absolutely, rain check it is," Sara said, trying to keep the relief out of her voice. "Thanks for doing this." She held out her hand for the folder, hating the lies. The deeper she got into this, the worse it seemed. For several moments she was sorely tempted to come clean to Cassie, bring her friends in on the situation and let Romo be furious with her. Was that really such a bad idea?

But when Cassie sketched a wave and headed for the door, Sara didn't call her back.

Instead, she closed and locked her sticky office door, and broke the seal on the folder. A quick scan confirmed the negative results on the DNA profiling, and added two critical pieces of information, one good, one bad. On the good side, the bullet hadn't come from an official weapon and it didn't match any of the personal sidearms belonging to task force officers, which suggested Romo hadn't been shot by one of the good guys. On the bad side, the spatter pattern—what Cassie had been able to get off the small pieces of black T-shirt, anyway—was consistent with close-range arterial spray from a severed throat, and the shirt's wearer had most likely wielded the knife.

Sara had taken a good look at the patterns on the shirt, and though she was no expert, she'd been certain that the blood from Romo's injury had soaked in atop the edges of the spatter, giving the incidents a time frame. Adding the information together, she could come up with a hypothesis of sorts, namely that sometime the prior day, just before—or during—the op that led to the manhunt, Romo had cut a man's throat and then been shot in the back by someone other than a cop.

Sara blew out a breath. Between the blood and bullet evidence, it seemed reasonable to conclude that Romo had been the unidentified man who had escaped alone from the manhunt. She tried to tell herself that didn't necessarily mean he was one of the good guys, but on some level it felt that way. He'd turned on the terrorists, or they'd turned on him. Either way, didn't it stand to reason that the enemy of Bear Claw's enemies was on their side, more or less?

The logic wasn't perfect, she knew, but she thought it might be enough to help her convince Romo to give himself up to Fax or Tucker, both of whom she trusted implicitly.

Her friends might not have liked him much after the breakup, but they were all task force members, and at this point would take whatever help they could get when it came to getting al-Jihad, Lee Mawadi, Jane Doe and the others into custody. They would help…assuming she could talk Romo into turning himself in. Problem was, he could be seriously stubborn, and Sara had never once been able to make him do something he didn't want to.

"You'd better start now," she told herself. "Lives might depend on it." Hers. His. Those of the citizens of Bear Claw.

Thinking fast, she turned to her computer, logged on to one of the larger international databases of medical literature and started keying in queries on retrograde amnesia, and techniques for retrieving blocked memories. She pulled together a basic information kit that gave her a few ideas on how she might be able to help Romo, and then started shutting down for the day. Stephen waved on his way out, having completed the agents' autopsies and filed the necessary reports. Once she was alone in the ME's office, Sara told herself she was okay, that there was no reason for her to feel exposed. This was her space, her place in the world.

For now, anyway. She'd just that morning received yet another of Proudfoot's aggrieved memos, warning that she needed to minimize her department's overtime. Which she'd be able to do if he let her hire another examiner, damn it.

That added stress dragged at her, worried her and had her jumping at shadows as she headed to her car. Although it was Saturday, the lot between the PD and ME's office was nearly full, mute evidence of the double and triple shifts being pulled by the members of the task force. She didn't see anyone else headed out, but felt a strange prickling between her shoulder blades, as though someone was watching her.

She took a look around as she unlocked her hybrid, checking out the windows of the buildings nearby, but didn't see anyone there, either. Under other circumstances, she would've brushed it off as her imagination, fueled by the manhunt and the pall of fear that hung citywide. Given what was going on in her life—and the fact that she'd promised Romo she would get an escort home—she dug out her cell phone and called Tucker's cell.

There was silence for a moment before he said, "Are you ready to tell me what's going on yet?"

Sara winced. "Cassie blabbed."

"We're worried. This isn't like you. If you're…" The tough homicide detective, who'd been only slightly domesticated by his marriage to forensic reconstruction specialist Alyssa Wyatt, paused as if feeling his way through delicate territory. "If you're trying to atone for something you think you should've done before, please don't. Leave the cloak-and-dagger stuff for the professionals. Okay?"

Sara's throat closed a little on the show of friendship and trust—he knew she was up to something, but wouldn't interfere directly. He just wanted her to know that he was there, that they all were, to help her. That was how it had been with Chelsea and Fax, she knew. The friends hadn't agreed with all of Chelsea's choices, but they'd been there when she'd needed them. Now they would do the same for Sara, the moment she asked. "Okay," she said, her voice a bare whisper. "I'll…okay."

"I'll follow you home myself. Just give me a couple of minutes." He hung up before she could respond to that, but he didn't mean anything by the hang-up. That was just Tucker's way.

Five minutes later, he was in his unmarked sedan, following her home, making her feel safe—for the moment, at least.

ROMO WOKE groggily at the sound of a key in the front door lock, found himself facedown on Sara's couch, and cursed himself for the weakness that had come from his injuries. He'd hated lying low, hoping to hell she was okay. But he'd had no choice. His body needed to heal, so he'd been forced to trust her not to turn him in, and not to take unnecessary risks.

He didn't need all of his memory back to know that trust wasn't something that came easily to him.

Cautiously, he levered himself upright on the sofa and then to his feet. He thought of meeting her at the door, but then he stopped himself. She'd promised to have one of her cop friends get her a police escort home. Logic said that—assuming her protection was any good—the cop would want to come inside and look around, making sure the house was clear. Hell, for all he knew, she'd had too long to think about the situation, and had made the logical decision to turn him in. In a way, he wouldn't blame her if she had.

Okay, that was a lie. He'd blame her, and he'd feel betrayed. But he'd get over it. He'd somehow gotten over her, hadn't he?

Hearing a low, masculine voice outside, he stiffened,

then ghosted down the hallway, toward the rear exit he'd scouted earlier. Granted, he could be in trouble if the house was surrounded. He had a feeling, though, that he could take care of a rear guard or two.

Sara might've been hoping that the spatter analysis would suggest he'd been standing next to the blood donor when the blow was struck, but in his gut he knew he'd been the one to make the fatal cut. He didn't know how he knew that, or how he knew it'd been a knife rather than a close-range gunshot. But he knew, damn it. Just as he knew Sara would be better off if he left now, if he just walked out the door and disappeared. Her friends would help keep her safe.

But who would help him?

The question had him pausing with his hand on the doorknob. Not because he was afraid of going off on his own—he had a feeling he was used to that. No, what had him hesitating was the knowledge that if Sara's most optimistic hypothesis was the right one, and he'd been undercover somehow, working for al-Jihad, then him disappearing was exactly the wrong move to make. If he'd been undercover, they needed to figure out his mission, who he'd been reporting to, and find a way to get back into the loop. He could have important information inside his skull, maybe even something that would blow the whole case wide open.

You're reaching, his inner cynic whispered. *The story sounds good, except for one thing. If you were undercover, why aren't you getting any memory flashes of that? All you're getting are the bad guys.*

He should go, he knew. But he'd hesitated too long.

"Leaving?" Sara's quiet voice said from the other end of the hallway leading to the back door.

She stood silhouetted in the light from the main room. The illumination picked out golden highlights in her shoulder-length hair and emphasized the long, lean length of her body in its smart power suit. She wore a long raincoat of mossy green against the damp, late-summer day, and the belted waist emphasized the narrowness of her waist, the femininity of the curves beneath. She looked expensive and put-together, and probably should have made him feel underdressed, in his borrowed sweatpants, T-shirt and bare feet. Instead, he was buffeted by an unfamiliar sense of rightness, a surge of "oh, there you are!" that made him want to cross to her, kiss her and welcome her home for the night.

And he so wasn't going there. Didn't dare. So instead of approaching her, he held his ground. "I wasn't taking off. I was preparing in case your cop came in with you and I needed to do a fast fade."

She made a quiet humming noise that didn't quite call him a liar, but said only, "Tucker offered to come in and take a look around, but I declined, and he took me at my word." She paused. "If you were going to vanish, you could've done it hours ago."

He thought about denying it, but figured there was little more than patchy honesty between them at this point, and he didn't have the heart to take that away from either of them. "I would have, but I passed out and only just now came around."

"Maybe that's your subconscious telling you to stay put."

"Maybe."

They stood squared off opposite each other for a long moment. Romo couldn't see her eyes, could only see the dark outline of her in the low, golden light, but he knew she was studying him, trying to figure him out. He wanted to tell her to let him know what she came up with, and he wouldn't have been kidding. He had a feeling she'd understood him better than he'd understood himself, even before the amnesia. But if that were the case, why had he cheated? He didn't feel like a cheat, didn't think it was his normal M.O. It didn't make any sense. None of it did.

"Well, it's your call. As usual." The last was said with a faint bite as she took a step back into the main room, ceding the hallway. The move brought her out of the shadows and into the light, showing him her lovely face, which was wearing an expression that was simultaneously both composed and worried. Her tone, though, was even as she said, "If it helps, neither the blood nor the bullet came from one of the officers or agents on the manhunt."

It did help, but he latched on to what she *hadn't* said. "The spatter was consistent with me cutting the victim's throat."

She swallowed. "Yes. How did you know?"

"I don't remember what happened," he said, answering the unspoken question. "It was just a feeling."

Unfortunately, feelings were all he had to go on just then, and they included his growing attraction for Sara, which was starting to mess with his ability to assess and analyze all the other things going on around them. He suspected the pull he felt toward her was a combination of unremembered history, the situation, and the simple fact that he'd been attracted to her once before, and nothing had changed about his basic taste. The things that had drawn them together before were still in place. And he suspected he wasn't the only one feeling the pull. He didn't know exactly what had happened during their breakup, or why, but he thought part of Sara might be seeing the situation as an opportunity for a do-over. Or maybe he was the one thinking that. Either way, asleep or awake, he was filled with thoughts of her, of how she had tasted when he'd kissed her, how she had felt against him.

Aware that they'd both been silent too long, he said, "I should go."

"Where?" The single word was both a question and a challenge, making him feel as though she'd just called him a coward.

"Away from you," he said bluntly, expecting her to take it personally, in a way wanting her to, because he didn't know how to deal with his almost obsessive need to be near her. It was a selfish, destructive urge, one he needed to fight. And in doing so, he attacked.

Instead of taking offense, she tilted her head and asked softly, "Does the idea of trusting someone frighten you that badly?"

Instincts had him wanting to snap at her that he wasn't afraid, but that would've been a lie. He *was* afraid, not so much for himself, but for her, for what he'd brought into her life. But he didn't snap. Instead, he moved away from the door and down the short hallway, crossing the distance between them and stopping just short of the light. "What do you suggest I do?"

"Let me set up a meeting," she said immediately. "You, me, Fax and Tucker. All the evidence points to you being undercover for the good guys, Romo. Let them help us figure out who you're working for."

"Your so-called evidence is pretty damned thin from where I'm standing," he said dryly. "All we really know for certain is that the clues we've got don't conclusively indicate that I killed those agents. Everything else is conjecture."

"I know you," she said staunchly. "You wouldn't have faked your own death to join al-Jihad. You're a good man."

"I cheated on you."

Her eyes flashed. "You're trying to make me kick you out. I won't do it."

"You should." He stepped into the light, into her space. He stopped opposite her, with a few feet separating them. He had the sensation of drowning as he looked down into her caramel-colored eyes. "Tell me to leave."

"Stay," she said instead. "Let me call Fax and Tucker."

He touched a finger beneath her chin and tipped her face up to his. "You believe in me that much," he murmured, "because of what we were to each other."

He knew touching her was a mistake the moment his fingertip connected with her soft skin. First, because of the warmth that spread up his arm and lodged in his chest, threatening to undo all his best intentions. And second, because her eyes snapped dark with what he thought was fury, but was wiped away before he could be sure, to be replaced by cool, studied indifference. She eased away. "Despite the impression you might have gotten from my kissing you last night, I'm all too aware of our history. Trusting you got me a broken heart before. This time it could very well get me killed."

He let his hand fall, held his palms up in apology. "Sorry. I misread."

"Yes. You did."

"Then why are you pushing me to stay and meet with your friends?"

"Because Bear Claw is my home," she said simply. "I won't let al-Jihad destroy it. I've hidden behind my job for too long, and it's time I stopped doing that. Which means that if there's something I can do to help the task force break the case, then by damn, I'm going to do it." She fixed him with a look that held more challenge than entreaty. "Will you?"

She was asking for the impossible. She wasn't just asking him to trust her, she was asking him to trust her friends, people he hadn't met in this incarnation of himself.

He nodded slowly. "Okay."

Surprise flared in her eyes. "You'll meet with Fax and Tucker?"

"Yeah. I'll meet with them." But even as he said the words, something inside him warned he was making a huge mistake.

Chapter Six

The next morning, Sara left the house early wearing a light suede jacket and casually elegant pants with a tailored shirt a couple of shades darker than her hair. Her boots were low-heeled and rubber-soled, and her purse, which she wore slung over her shoulder, was heavier than usual, containing the loaded .22, along with extra bullets. She'd tried to press the weapon on Romo, but he'd insisted that she be the one to carry the protection. Some small, soft part of her had wanted to believe his worry was personal, intimate.

They'd both slept in the living room the night before, for a second night in a row, she on the couch, he on his makeshift pallet near the door, keeping watch. Sometime during the night, though, he'd moved closer to her, and she'd awakened to find her fingertips dangling over the side of the couch just brushing his shoulder. It hadn't quite been his old habit of wanting some part of him touching some part of her, but it had been enough to make her heart shudder a little in her chest. Enough to make her yearn, damn him.

Focus! she told herself, forcing her attention on the meeting at hand as she marched to her hybrid and climbed inside.

The skin between her shoulder blades prickled with the sensation of watching eyes, but she told herself to ignore it. If al-Jihad's people had figured out where Romo was hiding, they wouldn't be sitting around, watching. They would've done something already. The thought brought a serious shiver, but it did make a fatalistic sort of sense. Which meant that if she was being watched, it wasn't by one of the terrorists. More than likely, she knew, it was Tucker. Or, since Tucker was due at their meeting point, he might have deputized Alyssa to keep watch in his stead. The married couple made a formidable team.

Sara had called Tucker first, then Fax, and had told them only that she needed to meet with them in the utmost secrecy. She hadn't dared reveal more than that, for fear that the information might leak to one of the conspirators believed to still be within the task force. Not that Fax or Tucker would talk, but still…thanks to Jane Doe's defection, al-Jihad's people had access to the latest spy-ware technology and strategy. As Fax had once said, the task force members had to assume that the terrorists had all of the toys and know-how the good guys did, and then some.

"Which is so *not* an encouraging thought," Sara muttered to herself as she fired up the hybrid's engine and pulled out of her driveway. After taking a few turns through her neighborhood and deciding she wasn't being followed, she drove down a street two blocks over from her house, and pulled up next to a thick stand of landscaped trees.

Romo slipped from concealment—she hadn't even seen him hiding there, though she'd been looking for him—and climbed into the hybrid, folding himself into the backseat and keeping his head down so it looked as though she were still alone. "See anything?" he asked as she pulled away from the bushes.

"Nope. But I'm not a professional, either."

"You do fine."

His calm assurance steadied her more than it probably should have. But then again, that was Romo. He'd always made her feel like more than she really was, as though together they made something that was better than each of them alone. She'd thought he'd felt the same way, until he'd proven otherwise. But although his betrayal was never far from the surface of her thoughts, she was startled to realize that the pain was beginning to fade, in a way it hadn't done during the months after they'd broken up, or after that, when she'd believed him dead. And that was a problem, she knew. Thanks to her mother, she was genetically and environmentally predisposed to forgive the man she loved, even when he patently didn't deserve forgiveness.

She could potentially get past Romo's disappearing act, presuming that he proved to have been undercover. They hadn't been together when he'd faked his death; he hadn't owed her an explanation or a warning, a sign that he was really alive. Or so she kept telling herself, and the logic worked even if the emotions lagged a little. What didn't work was knowing she was just as ready to forgive him for what had happened before then, when they *had* been together. All he'd had to do was send her some of his long, slow looks and a single hot, toe-curling kiss, and a large part of her was more than ready to forgive and forget, and give their relationship a second chance. Not that he'd even indicated that he wanted a second chance with her, she reminded herself. The weakness was inside her. It always had been.

"Problem?" he asked.

She glanced in the rearview mirror, saw him looking at her in it from his cramped position in the back. "Why would there be a problem?" she inquired with a faint bite in her tone as she returned her attention to the road. "My cheating ex comes back from the dead, bleeds all over my living room, forces me to lie to a friend and runs a strong risk of getting me killed. No problem there that I can see."

"All true, but none of it is news at this point. Which means there's something else going on in that head of yours that had you frowning." He paused. "You want to talk about it?"

"Not even remotely," she snapped.

"I'll listen. Venting might help."

She cut her eyes back to his in the mirror. "And that's the sort of thing that leaves no question you've got a head injury and amnesia. The old Romo Sampson never would've put himself in the line of fire for an emotional outburst." He'd avoided negative emotions, claiming he got enough of them at work; he didn't need to go looking for drama on his off hours.

"I'm starting to think I might not have entirely liked the old me," Romo said mildly.

"Join the club." But the absurdity of it tugged a reluctant smile from her as she turned onto the highway and then off it again.

She made a quick stop at one of the big box stores that dotted the region, and went inside to buy jeans, a white oxford and a black blazer for Romo, so he didn't have to wear her sweatpants to the meeting. He'd kept hold of his own boots, so she filled in the gaps with a package of socks and a pair of boxers. The clothes weren't the more expensive brands he'd preferred, but once he'd changed in the car—covering the winces as best he could, though obviously still in pain—he looked much more like the man he'd once been, albeit a version of himself wearing a layer of stubble and a hunted, haunted look in the back of his eyes.

Haggard or not, Romo's dark, sharp good looks had always drawn female attention wherever he went. And, damn it, his looks hadn't changed with the time away. If anything, his features had gotten even sharper with the loss of a few pounds, as though any softness that had once been inside him had been burned away by whatever he'd seen and done. *And it's that "whatever he's seen or done" that you need to focus on,* she reminded herself, forcing her eyes away from the mirror and gluing them back on the road.

She hadn't thought he'd noticed her glance. But moments later, he said softly, "I'm sorry I've made things so difficult for you, Sara."

He saw through her, damn it, saw into her. He knew

what she was thinking and feeling, and the knowledge made her feel stripped raw inside. But when she glanced into the mirror and away, she saw only compassion in his gorgeous green eyes with their ridiculously long, sexy lashes. "Just don't kiss me again," she said, voice going ragged before she could force it steady.

She expected easy assent. Instead, he said, "I can't promise that."

The quiet statement sent a bolt of electricity through her midsection as she rolled to a stop at a red light. She wanted to turn and look at him directly, but didn't dare, so she met his eyes once again in the mirror, and saw heat there. Desire. "Don't," she said, the single word coming out in a dry-mouthed whisper.

"I'm not the guy who cheated on you, Sara." His eyes were steady on hers.

"Yes, you are." But she knew that was a lie. The old Romo had been a charming rogue who'd committed himself fiercely to the chase once she'd let him know that she was attracted to him but made it a point not to date men who went through girlfriends with depressing regularity. She'd eventually given in and gone out with him, then had fallen for him, but he'd only let himself fall so far. There had been a distance between them, a barrier she'd been unable to breach.

With this man, though, there was no barrier that she could see. Stripped of his practiced game, he remained as fiercely protective of her as he'd been before, but he let her see it in him. His eyes showed his thoughts and feelings, and when he reached up between the front seats to touch her elbow in a brief caress that lit her body as though it had been so much more, there was an honesty in his touch that she didn't remember from before. It was as though, in losing himself, Romo Sampson had found a new, different man. A better one.

"Sara," he began.

"We're here," she interrupted, unable to deal with whatever he was about to say, knowing she wanted to hear it far too much. She turned into the small parking lot of the state park trailhead that Fax had chosen as a meeting place and saw two other cars already there, a dark green truck and a standard-issue sedan. "Those are Fax and Tucker's rides."

As she rolled the hybrid to a stop, Fax emerged from his truck. A couple of inches under six feet, he was tough and compact, with dark hair, piercing blue eyes and a thin scar running through one eyebrow. He looked healthier than he had when Sara had first met him, fresh out of his own undercover hell. He hadn't mellowed over the ten months, though, despite his engagement to Chelsea. If anything, Fax had grown even more intense as she had progressed through her FBI training, as though he was bound and determined to end al-Jihad's reign of terror before the woman he loved wound up any deeper in the danger. Even now, he practically vibrated with deadly tension as he rounded his truck to join Tucker, who leaned back against his car, arms folded over his broad chest.

Tucker was a couple of inches taller than Fax, with wavy dark hair, brown eyes and a swarthy tan and an air of unconstrained wildness that made him look more like a park ranger than a senior homicide detective.

Both men wore bulletproof vests marked with their

affiliations, and had guns on their hips. When Sara parked the hybrid and just sat there for a second, dithering, her friends moved to stand shoulder to shoulder, presenting a strong, united front. She told herself she should feel reassured by the sight. Instead, nerves skittered to life beneath her skin.

"They're going to kill me when they hear what I've done," she said, mostly to herself.

"They're not going to touch you," Romo said succinctly from the backseat, where he was still hunkered down, avoiding detection. "And for the record, the you-and-me conversation isn't over."

Her throat went dry even as her blood revved in her veins. "What if I want it to be over?"

"I can't let it be over," he said, and in his eyes she saw a raw honesty she'd never seen in his face before. "I don't know what the old me did, exactly, and I sure as hell don't understand why he did what he did, but I'm not that man anymore, Sara. And the man I am now wants his chance with you."

Her heart thudded unevenly in her chest. "I don't do second chances."

"It wouldn't be a second chance. It'd be a first one for the guy I am now."

A bubble of near-hysterical laughter rose within her. "For how long? As far as I know, you're thirty seconds from being dragged back undercover. And even if that doesn't happen, how long will it be until it all comes back, until the real Romo Sampson returns?"

"Trust me," he said. "I won't let you down this time. I promise."

But how could she trust him when she didn't really know who he was anymore? Before she could respond—before she could even figure out how she wanted to respond, as warmth and wishes swirled in her chest—he straightened up and slipped from the vehicle, leaving the door ajar as he headed toward where Fax and Tucker both went stiff and on point at the sight of him.

"Sampson!" Tucker bit off. "Son of a—"

Heart drumming, Sara hurried to catch up with Romo. They were maybe three or four car lengths from the men, and Sara could already feel the tension coming off them in waves. Figuring she should make a rear-guard effort to smooth things over, she called, "Hey, you two. Thanks for meet—"

A whistling shriek cut her off, followed quickly by Romo's shout of alarm. Then he was slamming into her, driving her to the ground.

Half a heartbeat later, the world exploded.

They'd been ambushed! Sara's heart constricted in her chest as Romo covered her body with his own. "No!" she cried. "Tucker! Fax!" She tried to struggle out from beneath Romo, but he wouldn't budge, just hung on to her tightly, covering her ears with his big, strong hands.

A terrible noise blasted over them, coming from where Fax's truck had been. Waves of concussion battered Sara, even though she was protected by Romo's weight pressing her down into the hard surface of the parking area.

Her ears rang and went dull as panic gripped her, took her over, paralyzing in its intensity. She thought someone was screaming, realized a moment later it was her, and shut up. Heat flared in the air, bringing terrible, choking smoke.

Slitting her eyes, she looked toward the conflagration. Fax's truck was burning. Tucker's car was marked with blast char, its front quarter panel mangled. The two men lay twenty or so feet away from the vehicles, close to each other. Neither was moving.

"Fax! Tucker!" Hacking against the burning ash, Sara struggled to get up, to get to her friends. Then Romo rolled off her, dragged her up and pulled her into a shambling run. Only he was going in the wrong direction. He was headed away from the other men.

"No!" Sara dug in her heels and tried to twist away. "No, we've got to go back for them!"

"We can't." His grip was inexorable, his jaw set and his face colder than she'd ever seen it, even before the amnesia, when he'd been a far harder man.

"Romo, stop. We can't leave them." Tears stung her eyes, a combination of smoke and emotion.

"We don't have a choice. Move!" He shoved her into the back of the hybrid, shut the door and climbed in the driver's seat. He had the little vehicle moving before she even scrambled to grab the door handle with some mad intent of flinging herself out and running to Fax's and Tucker's aid.

She froze as a second missile whistled through the air and impacted the spot where the hybrid had been. The parking area cratered in an instant, and the little car rocked with the waves of concussion, but the tires held and the hybrid leaped away, engine racing as

Romo gunned it out of the parking lot. Sara clung to the door handle as the little vehicle flew away from the attack.

"Call it in," he snapped, attention divided between the road ahead and that behind them. "Tell them to get to Tucker and Fax ASAP, but don't say anything about us."

Mind blank with fear, Sara scrabbled for her pocket, pulling out her cell. She stabbed the familiar number and reported the attack in a voice that cracked with tears. When the dispatcher asked her name, she started to say, "This is Sara—"

"Give me that." Romo grabbed her cell and tossed it out the driver's-side window.

"What the hell?" she demanded angrily.

"You made your call. They'll get to Fax and Tucker in time, thanks to you. But we can't let them track the phone."

"Who, the cops?" Incredulity had her voice cracking, but inside her, sluggish fear stirred. "Romo, at this point we *want* the cops to find us. Don't you get it? Al-Jihad's people just tried to kill us to keep us from talking to Fax and Tucker." Her throat closed as the sight of their motionless bodies flashed in her head. "And now they're…"

"Stunned," he filled in when she faltered. "They'll be okay."

"We left them there!" she snapped, anger rising quickly. "What if the shooters go after them, to finish them off?"

"They won't." His voice rang with calm assurance.

"How do you know?"

"Because that's them behind us." He nodded into the rearview mirror.

That was when she realized he didn't have the engine redlined anymore; he'd eased up on the gas, though he kept steady progress up onto the highway, weaving through the sparse Sunday morning traffic.

Maybe a half mile back, there was another car making similar moves.

Sara's blood iced in her veins. "You're letting them *catch* us?"

He slid her a sardonic glance. "If they'd wanted to catch us, they would've by now. This putt-putt car of yours isn't exactly a hot rod."

She craned her neck. "Then what are they doing?"

"That's what I'm trying to figure out." He grimaced as he drove. "They aimed for the cops' vehicles, not the cops, and they didn't take a second shot at us, which they damn well had the time to do. Which means they were trying to break up the meeting without killing us—or more likely without killing me, no offense."

"None taken," she said grimly, as her mind moved ahead to the next logical conclusion. "You have something they want. Or at least they think you do. And they don't want the cops to have it."

"What's more, nobody followed us from your place," he pointed out, voice all but expressionless as he pulled off the highway at a random exit somewhere south of Bear Claw. "Which means that either the guys with the RPG were working with your friends—"

"They're not."

"—or," he continued as though she hadn't interrupted, "they found out about the meeting through your friends."

"Neither Fax nor Tucker would've said anything," she maintained.

"For all we know, they're being monitored. Or else someone on the inside recognized the samples you gave to the forensic analyst and put her and her contacts under surveillance."

That made sense, Sara realized. "But if that were the case, wouldn't they have been watching me?"

"Maybe they hadn't gotten there yet," he said, grimly navigating the hybrid through a set of back roads she didn't recognize. "You might not have been first on the list of people I'd go to, given that you're not a cop."

"But we had a relationship," she pointed out. "They would've looked at me eventually."

"True." He paused. "Maybe they did follow us from your place, after all. But if they knew where I'd been, why didn't they move in on me sooner? What the hell are they waiting for?"

"Maybe for you to complete your mission, whatever it was," Sara said cautiously.

"Damn it," he said, which she took as his way of saying she was right. But when he let up on the gas, she realized that wasn't the only thing bothering him.

"What's wrong?"

He turned haunted eyes toward her. "Two things. One, when we turned off, the chase car kept going on the highway. And two, I recognize this neighborhood."

Her stomach clenched into a hard, hurting knot. She looked around them and saw nothing familiar; she'd never been there with him, didn't know of any reason why he would recognize the area. They were maybe a half hour south of Bear Claw, in a typical suburban area that had little to distinguish it aside from its lack of distinguishing characteristics. This close to the highway, there were fast food and coffee shop drive-throughs on just about every corner, liquor and convenience stores, and a variety of more specialized shops. As they moved farther away from the highway, the commercial strip gave way to modest houses and multifamily dwellings, some in decent shape, others tending toward shabby.

It wasn't the sort of place the Romo she'd known would have hung out. But the man he'd become drove with quiet self-assurance, clearly knowing the way to his destination. Whatever that was.

Swallowing hard, she said, "You're starting to remember what happened to you?"

"Not remembering, precisely. But I know the way." He let the hybrid roll to a stop and pointed up and across a couple of blocks. "See that one up there, with the falling-down awning over the window? I'm pretty sure I lived there."

"Not while I knew you," she said immediately.

"No. Not then. After." His eyes were hard and remote, his jaw locked, his body language somehow more aggressive even though he was simply sitting in the driver's seat.

He looked like a dangerous stranger. The realization warned Sara that for the first time since the day before, she wasn't so sure of Romo's innocence. Their attackers had let him live, gunning down Fax and Tucker instead. But why?

"Either they need something from me, or they still think I'm on their side," he said, as though she'd asked aloud. Then again, it stood to reason that the question would be at the forefront of both of their minds.

Sara blew out a breath. "Were those men chasing you, or herding you, making sure you went where they wanted?"

"Damned if I know."

An icy chill shivered through her. "Which means they could be waiting for you in that house."

"I know." Parking the hybrid where they sat, he unhooked his seat belt. "Stay here. I'm going to check it out." He glanced at her. "I have to know."

She opened her mouth to argue, but could tell from his expression there was nothing she could say to change his mind. Reaching into her coat pocket, she pulled out the revolver and held it out to him. "Take this."

He stilled and looked at her, eyes dark. "You're sure?"

"Positive." It was a gesture of faith in the absence of evidence. She thought they both needed it.

He took the weapon, his fingers grazing hers. "Thanks."

"Be careful."

He left the engine running and she stayed put as he climbed out and sauntered along the sidewalk, past the house he'd indicated and then around the back. He reappeared a few minutes later at the front door, did something with the lock—she didn't think she wanted to know what he'd done or where he'd learned to do it—and let himself in.

There was no sign of anyone waiting for him, at least not that she could see as the door swung shut at his back, leaving her staring once again at the house. She told herself to stay put, told herself to do as he'd ordered. He was the professional; he knew what he was talking about. She'd be safer in the hybrid, and he'd be safer in the house if he didn't have to think about protecting her.

It was all very logical, all very reasonable. And the arguments were still spooling through her head as she killed the engine, pocketed the key, locked the doors and headed across the street.

ROMO HELD HIMSELF TENSE and wary as he moved into the house, somewhat disappointed to find it empty. He'd been looking forward to pounding on someone who had the answers he sought. Since there wasn't anyone to "question," he was left with the house itself. Unfortunately, it'd been stripped of whatever personal touches it had once possessed. The single sad and lonely piece of décor was a heavily framed picture in the kitchen, showing an insipid child holding a sunflower.

He'd lived there, no question about it. He'd known how to jimmy the lock without effort, had known where to push on the dead bolt to pop it loose. He knew that the short entryway hall opened into a TV room with stained wall-to-wall carpeting and mismatched secondhand furniture, with a dingy kitchen beyond. He knew that the two doors off the main room led to a bedroom on the right, a bathroom on the left. But beyond those location-based memories, he didn't know jack.

The rooms held little more than basic furniture. There was no sign of how long he'd stayed there, whether alone or with company, and what he—or they—had done there.

"Come on, come on," he chivvied his brain, trying to remember something, anything. He had a feeling that all he needed to do was pull up one viable memory on command, and the rest would cascade from there. But recall remained stubbornly out of reach, leaving him frustrated and adrift.

He was acutely conscious of time passing, the weight of the gun in his pocket and the knowledge that Sara was sitting outside in her silly little car, unprotected. He had to get back to her, and make sure the guys in the chase car were really gone. Before the explosion he would've seriously considered heading out the back and disappearing. His shoulder was sore but usable, his head clear. Even Sara had admitted he was strong enough to go off on his own. But there was no way he could leave her now. Their attackers had seen her, had probably known all along that Romo had gone to her for help. They'd just been biding their time. Question was, how much longer would that last? He feared the answer would be "not long."

"What is the damned mission?" he muttered, crossing the room and sticking his head in the bathroom, then the bedroom. "Why did they want me here?" At first when the car had peeled off the chase, he'd assumed there would be someone waiting for him at his destination, some sort of information, or a threat. But the utter emptiness of the place didn't make any sense.

Unless there's a message, he thought out of nowhere.

He wasn't sure whether a memory clicked in his brain, or if it was just the one thing that jarred in the whole place, but he moved back into the main room, crossed to the kitchen and stood staring at the hideous print of the smirking child holding the half-wilted sunflower. He felt around the edge of the picture frame, thinking it might conceal a safe. It turned out to be nothing more than a frame hanging on a bent nail, but his fingers found a flat button on one edge.

Just as he pressed the button, the doorknob turned and the front door swung inward.

Swearing, he palmed the revolver and had it trained on the doorway as a lean, elegant figure stepped through, hands raised.

"It's just me," Sara said, shutting the door at her back. "I couldn't sit there any longer. Find anything?"

Before he could curse her for startling him, for walking into a situation she wasn't trained to deal with or for just generally making him crazy, a new voice interjected, coming from the kitschy, message-recording picture frame.

"You have something we need, Sampson." The voice was cool and sharply enunciated, and came with a sense of cold, reptilian violence. Without knowing how he knew, Romo was certain it was al-Jihad. The recording continued. *"We've left you free this long because we're giving you a chance to do the right thing. Deliver the stolen information to me within forty-eight hours of this message. If you do not, the people you once cared for will be killed, one at a time, until you do…starting with*

Dr. Whitney. Agent Fairfax and Detective McDermott were a warning. We can get to anyone, any time we want. Remember that when you try to figure out whose side you're really on."

Romo cursed bitterly, helplessly, as the recording ended. Not looking at Sara, he punched the button again, but somehow it had been jimmied to be a one-time-only message. Not that he really needed or wanted to hear it again. The words, and the threats, were burned into his cortex.

"Did you…" Sara began, then trailed off. Swallowing audibly, she tried again. "Who was that? Do you know what he's talking about?"

"It was al-Jihad," he grated, turning on her. "And he wants information. But what information? And where the hell am I supposed to deliver it?"

"We need to figure that out pronto," she said pragmatically. Her eyes were hollow with fear and her lower lip trembled faintly, but she didn't weep or wail. It might've been easier if she did, because then maybe he could've packed her off into protective custody in defiance of the terrorist's claim that he could get to anyone, anywhere. Surely she'd be safer with her own people than with him? But that was just it, he knew. They didn't have a clue yet who was safe and who wasn't. More, he was rapidly losing confidence that he could keep Sara safe, at the same time that her safety was becoming paramount to him.

She shamed him. She humbled him. And damned if he didn't think he was falling for her all over again.

Chapter Seven

Desperate for a status report on Fax and Tucker, Sara directed Romo to one of the area's ubiquitous convenience stores and bought a cheap disposable cell phone.

As Romo pulled them away from the curb and headed the hybrid back toward the city, Sara dialed Chelsea's number, her throat closing when Chelsea answered on the third ring. Chelsea had been Sara's employee and friend. And Sara had nearly gotten her fiancé killed.

"Hello?" Chelsea repeated.

"Chels," Sara said softly. *Do you know that it was my fault?* she thought, but didn't say.

There was a moment of stunned silence, then a long, shuddering exhale. "Sara." There was a wealth of relief and grief in the word.

"How are they? Are they going to be okay?" Sara's voice broke as grief, guilt and tears clogged her throat.

"I'm on my way to the hospital now—" Chelsea broke off, clearing her throat. "They're both going to be okay. Fax was stunned and knocked around, and cracked a couple of ribs. They're watching him for internal bleeding, but the outlook is good."

Sara's lungs had locked on the recitation, as the list of Fax's injuries brought home just what a terrible situation they were in. She'd wanted to hear "he's fine, just got the wind knocked out of him." It was what she'd expected for a man who'd always seemed a little larger than life, even back when she'd first met him and none of them—except Chelsea, of course—had been certain he was the deep-cover agent he claimed, instead of the fugitive the law considered him. For a man like Fax to be laid low…it was almost inconceivable.

"What about Tucker?" she whispered, tears blurring her vision.

"He's in surgery."

Sara's heart constricted and she stifled a sob. "I'm so sorry."

"It's not your fault," Chelsea said. "They were following up on something for the task force and wound up ambushed."

She didn't know, Sara realized. Fax hadn't told her that she'd been the one to set up the meeting. Then again, it stood to reason. She'd demanded the utmost secrecy from both Fax and Tucker. They hadn't even told their wives.

For a moment, Sara was tempted to confess everything. But then she thought of the recorded message and its overt threat. She had put Fax and Tucker in the terrorists' crosshairs by setting up the meeting. She wasn't going to repeat that mistake and endanger any more of her friends.

"I'm almost to the hospital," Chelsea said. "Are you on your way?"

"No," Sara said softly. "I'm not. But believe me, I want to be there."

There was a moment of silence before Chelsea's voice changed and she said, "Sara, what's wrong?"

"I've got to go." Sara gripped the phone tightly, wishing there was another way but not seeing it. "Tell Cassie…when you see her, tell Cassie to check those fabric samples again for a sebaceous donor. She'll understand."

"That's good, because I don't," Chelsea said, her voice gaining a note of pique. "If you're in some sort of trouble—"

"I'll be fine," Sara interrupted with a lie. "Just tell her. And tell Fax and Tucker I'm praying for them." She hung up before she lost her nerve entirely, glancing at Romo. "Fax is okay. Tucker's in surgery."

He didn't say anything, just reached across the space separating them and gripped her hand briefly in support. The gesture served only to remind her that they were, from that point forward, on their own.

"We can't go to anyone else for help," she said dully. The need and necessity of avoiding the people she cared about clutched at her, digging in claws of concern. "It's too dangerous." She glanced at him. "Cassie will find your DNA in whatever sweat deposits were left on that shirt. It'll take a couple of days, though, because they'll be focusing on the scene of the blast. By then it might not matter, because as soon as Fax and Tucker wake up, they'll remember seeing you."

"We hope," Romo said with a vague gesture to his own skull.

"I've been thinking about that," Sara began.

He cut a look at her. "Go on. What are you thinking, hypnosis?"

"Close, but not quite," she said, forcing her mind back on the practicalities when fear and grief threatened to swamp her. "I don't see you as being all that susceptible. I was thinking more along the lines of sodium thiopental."

That got his attention. "Is that anything like sodium pentothal?"

She nodded. "Same thing, different name."

"Where were you planning on finding truth serum?"

"The hospital." At his sharp look, she elaborated, "It's only a truth serum on TV and in the movies, really. Us medical types prefer to think of it as the first step in general anesthesia." She paused, and when he didn't say anything, continued. "There's no guarantee it'll do anything but really relax you, making you more likely to talk. But if the memories are close to coming through, what could it hurt?"

His mouth twisted in a wry grimace. "What, indeed?" He sent her a long, slow look. "You sure you want to hear my stream of consciousness?"

Aware that his mood had gone suddenly dark, more so even than before, she frowned. "What are you afraid you'll say?"

"I don't know," he said grimly. "But I don't want you to...despise me."

I won't, she started to say, but didn't because she

wasn't sure that was something she could promise. What would she do if he described himself murdering someone in cold blood? She wasn't sure she could handle that, whether or not the victim was one of the terrorists. So instead of going with the quick, too-easy lie, she went with the truth. "We'll deal with whatever happens, Romo. It's not like you're trying to impress me, right?"

He shot her an unreadable look. "What if I am?"

"Then trust me enough to let me load you up with truth serum." She'd intended for it to sound flip, but somehow it didn't. It came out more like a challenge. A test.

After a moment, he nodded. "Okay."

"Okay?" It wasn't until that moment she realized she hadn't really expected him to go along with the idea. New man or not, Romo wasn't the sort of guy who'd willingly strip himself bare…at least not mentally.

Despite everything, though, it was the passing thought of him stripping himself physically that stuck in her head as he drove them to the second of two area hospitals where she had staff privileges as a pathologist. She knew it was probably transference, her brain's efforts to distract her from thinking about less pleasant topics. And, as they went over the simple plan and Romo parked the hybrid in the hospital's guest lot, she decided to go with the delicious mental image. She was doing what needed to be done, damn it. She deserved a nice moment.

Thinking that, and thinking she could very well be

down to forty-six or so hours of safety based on the timeline in al-Jihad's threat, she leaned across the small car and touched her lips to Romo's. The kiss was brief, though suffered nothing in the way of warmth or zing. And when she pulled away, she saw the same knowledge in his eyes.

"For luck," she said.

"For luck," he echoed, and pressed the revolver into her hand.

She recoiled a little and would've insisted that he keep the weapon, but knew he had a point. Al-Jihad had given Romo two days to find and deliver the stolen information—whatever the hell it was—but that didn't mean he wouldn't take Sara beforehand, as added pressure. Not to mention that the task force was going to figure out her involvement sooner or later.

She forced her lips into a smile. "Lucky for me this particular hospital doesn't have a metal detector on the way in."

"Even more reason for you to take the gun," he said grimly. "You've got ten minutes." His expression made it clear that he hated the plan, even though they'd been unable to come up with one that would keep them together while she snuck into the hospital and filched the necessary supplies. "If you're not back out here by then, I'm coming in after you."

"Don't come in," she said, because they'd been over the idea already. "You won't be able to get past the front desk without ID, which you don't have because you're dead. I, on the other hand, have all the right identification. I'll be fine." She hoped.

Leaving him to stew in the car, she headed to the staff entrance of the medical center. She couldn't go to the larger city hospital, because that was where Fax and Tucker had been taken. It was sure to be swarming with task force members who would wonder why she wasn't with her friends, waiting for word on the injured men. So the medical center it was. She'd spent far less time there than at the hospital, but she was there every week or so, helping with on-site pathology when the occasion called for it. She knew her way around well enough. As an added benefit, the center was weekend busy, with more walk-in cases than doctors to handle them.

The resulting semicontrolled chaos meant she was able to slip in, find an unattended anesthesia station and relieve it of enough sodium thiopental to do the job, along with a handful of syringes and needles in their sterile packages. She felt bad knowing that the anesthesiologist in charge of the station was going to have to account for the missing items, but this wasn't the time for niceties. She'd lied to her friends; it seemed a short leap to outright theft from strangers.

It's for a good cause, she told herself as she ghosted back out of the medical center well within her ten-minute time window. *Everyone in Bear Claw—everyone who isn't a conspirator, anyway—wants to get al-Jihad back behind bars.* But as she crossed the parking lot to where Romo was waiting for her, she couldn't help wondering whether she was making excuses, looking for reasons to forgive him, excuses to reconcile what he'd done with the fact that despite it all, she was still desperately attracted to him. It would certainly fit her personal pattern.

"All set?" he said the moment she opened the door.

"Got it." Deciding she'd deal with all the doubts later, she slipped into the driver's seat. "Let's get out of here."

"Where to?"

"Someplace safe." She didn't care where they went, she realized as he pulled out of the parking lot. She leaned back in the seat and closed her eyes for a second. When she did that, she could see the explosion all over again, could hear it ringing in her ears. Fax had suffered broken ribs, Tucker more than that. Her fault, she knew. All hers. And the terrorists', of course, but if she'd called for help the moment she'd walked into her home and seen a man bleeding to death on her living room carpet, none of this would have happened.

"Hey." Romo touched her hand. "You okay?"

"Just torturing myself with a little game of 'what if.'"

"Like 'what if you'd gone into surgery like your mother wanted?'"

She smiled, her eyes still closed. "Yeah. Something like that." Then she stilled, and opened her eyes. Looked at him. "I didn't tell you my mother wanted me to be a surgeon."

He glanced away from the road and met her eyes, frowning. "Yes, you did. You—" He broke off, shaking his head. "It's gone now."

The suspicions she'd mostly managed to set aside crept back around the edges of her consciousness. "You're remembering more and more. Are you sure you want to go through with this?"

He cut her a sharp look. "Are you asking whether I'm

faking the amnesia? Seems like a moot point, given what you're about to inject me with. In about a half hour, you'll be able to ask me whatever you want and be certain of getting a real answer."

"According to some studies, the pentothal only works as well as it does is because subjects believe it'll compel them to tell the truth, so they do. Really, all it does is lower your inhibitions. It doesn't make you any less likely to lie."

"Are you saying you think I've been playing you all along?" Romo's voice was a low growl.

Sara's chest went tight, but she held her ground. "Fax and Tucker are in the hospital right now because of me. Cut me some slack, will you?"

He drove in silence for a few minutes, then exhaled a long breath before he said, "You've got an odd habit of straddling the line. I wonder if that wasn't what had me looking so hard at your office in my previous life."

She stiffened, stung. "What exactly do you mean by that?"

"I think you know, but let me give you a couple of examples…like how you've hidden me but dropped a raft of hints to your friends. Or how you've gotten involved with the task force, but not really. How you practice medicine, but not really. It seems to me that you do a whole lot of things in your life halfway. Then when they don't work out, you can content yourself with knowing you didn't try your hardest, so you didn't really fail, while at the same time, you failed, which means you were justified in not trying your hardest." He wasn't looking at her now, was concentrating on the road as he said, "I can't help wondering whether that wasn't part of what happened between the two of us. I might've screwed up, but how hard did you fight to keep us together, really?"

Her blood had chilled in her veins as he'd been talking, turning icy with anger, and betrayal. "How *dare* you?" she snapped. "Over the past two days, I've patched you up, I've hidden you, I've helped you above and beyond the call of whatever might've been between us in the past. If you don't call that me giving my all, then nuts to you. I don't need you, and I don't need your grief." Her voice roughened on angry tears. "And for your information, I didn't fight worth a damn to keep us together, because do you know what? I spent my childhood watching my otherwise intelligent mother take my cheating father back time after time. I heard all the excuses she made to herself, and to me. So forgive me if I don't do excuses anymore, and I don't beat my head against walls, or however you define giving something my all. If that means that I've been giving up on things by your definition, then fine, I give up. But only on goals and people that haven't given me any reason to fight for them." *Like you.*

She didn't say the last two words aloud, but they hung in the air between them as he turned off the highway and headed them into one of the long-term parking lots at the airport. They didn't speak again as he collected his ticket from the automated machine, and found an out-of-the-way space for the little hybrid. Once he'd killed the engine, they sat in silence for a moment, in the dim illumination of the badly lit garage.

"I'm nervous," he said finally.

It was the last thing she would've expected him to be feeling, never mind admitting it, that she just sat there a moment longer. "You're afraid of what you're going to remember? What you might've done?"

He nodded, jaw clenching and unclenching before his expression firmed once again. "Well, putting it off isn't going to change the past, is it?"

She shook her head. "Not in my experience, no."

"Then let's go." They locked up the hybrid, abandoning it for the time being in the long-term lot, knowing that sooner or later the task force was going to start looking for her, and they needed just under two days of space to do what they needed to do. They took a shuttle to the terminal, another to a nearby hotel, where they caught a cab to another airport hotel. There, figuring they'd muddied their trail sufficiently, they rented connecting rooms using the cash she'd pulled from an ATM when she'd bought the disposable phone.

By unspoken consent, they both went straight into his room. It was a supremely generic midscale hotel room, complete with mirrored closet doors, a generous marble-and-chrome bathroom, and a main room done in greens and browns, with a big king-size bed and bank of wide windows overlooking the parking lot.

Romo flicked on the lights, then crossed to the window and closed the curtains. He turned to her, seeming larger somehow than he had only moments before, his presence commanding her attention, her imagination. "Did we ever travel together?" he asked, his voice low and rough, almost wistful.

She shook her head. "No. We stayed close to home."

He grimaced. "Pity. I would've liked to be the sort of guy who took his girl down to Cancun for the weekend, just because."

You could be, she almost said, but the words wound up stuck in her throat because she wasn't sure that was the truth. If the pentothal worked and he regained his memory, he'd go back to being the man she'd almost loved, the one who hadn't loved her back. It didn't seem realistic to hope that he'd retain the more open, giving personality he'd shown her over the past few days. That wasn't Romo. It was…a fantasy, she supposed. A nice wish. The man who could've loved her back. The man, she thought, she would've fought for.

He smiled sadly, as though she'd said the words aloud. "Yeah. No second chances, right?"

"Right." She waved him to the single king-size bed. "Get comfortable."

He tried to send her a suggestive leer, but it fell flat. So instead he took a deep breath, toed off his shoes, shrugged out of his blazer and lay facedown on the bed, close to the edge of the mattress. She killed the room lights, leaving the small space lit only by the dim, indirect illumination coming from the bathroom. Then she pulled the desk chair up close to him, loaded a syringe, bared the crook of his elbow and injected the liquid into his vein with little ceremony.

As she did so, she hoped to hell she'd gotten the dosage right. Pentothal was a barbiturate, which meant if she dosed him too heavily, he'd fall asleep instead of remembering. So she went very light on the dose, thinking she could add if she needed to.

She thought she'd come close to getting it right, though. Within a few minutes, his eyes started going unfocused. His eyelids drooped and he looked at her with fuzzy good humor. "Am I remembering anything?" he said, voice blurry.

"You tell me," she said.

He smiled goofily. "Tell you what?"

The silly, too-open expression on his normally grim-edged face made her heart turn over in her chest, made her soul whisper, *Oh, Romo.* But she knew she couldn't let that show, couldn't let him know how close she was to falling all over again, for a man who didn't really exist.

ROMO WAS FLOATING on something warm and soft, surrounded by golden light, with an angel hovering over him. On one level, he knew he was in an airport hotel, that the angel was Sara and he was stoned on barbiturates. On another level, though, he was someone else, someone he didn't recognize. That man was closed and unhappy, angry with himself, untrusting of the world. He hoped that wasn't the real him. If it was, he didn't think he was going to like the guy very much.

The thought brought a pang of unease, a slash of grief, because now he better understood Sara's reluctance to give him a second chance. He couldn't blame her if this was the guy she'd dated, the guy who'd broken her heart. Romo would've fought the bastard if he knew how. He didn't, though, which meant that all he could do was howl in silent anguish as that dark, angry part of him overtook the man he'd been for the past few days.

The world darkened around him, grew dim and unhappy.

As if from far away, he heard Sara ask, "Do you remember the prison riot?"

Yes, he remembered. And he wished to hell he didn't, because the moment the floodgates cracked, the memories started spilling back. Shock rattled through him, tempered with excitement at the thought that finally— finally!—they were getting somewhere.

He could picture his contact, the man who'd recruited him as a code cracker, tempting him with promises of money and all the computer power he could want. The guy had said there wouldn't be any killing except for Romo's faked death and the subsequent body switch, which would be covered up by conspirators within the various organizations. The man had lied, though. Several guards and prisoners had died, along with the prison warden himself.

But then something seriously weird happened—the moment those images flashed in his reconnecting brain, they morphed to another scene entirely, one of rainy darkness and a blood-drenched alleyway. And a woman lying sprawled inelegantly on the street, her throat cut, her eyes staring up at him in accusation.

Where were you? her eyes demanded. *Why didn't you save me?*

Nausea and horror twisted through him as the rest of it came back. And he wished to hell he'd left it buried.

Chapter Eight

One second Romo was lying quietly, and the next, he arched back on the bed, his hands fisting in the covers and his face etching with horror.

"Alicia!" he cried. The word seemed torn from his throat, a single word of anguish, of despair.

Sara froze. "Romo?" she whispered. "What's wrong? What are you seeing?"

Ugly suspicions took root, bringing a flare of jealousy. Had he started a relationship under his postfuneral identity, whatever it had been? What had happened to the woman? From the sound of his voice and the pain on his face, it hadn't been good. Trying to calm the rapid gallop of her heart, telling herself it might be important, no matter how much it hurt to hear that he'd found someone after her, Sara made herself ask, "Who is Alicia?"

"Detective Alicia Frey." His eyes were closed, his face carved with terrible pain. "She was my partner back in Vegas, before I came to Bear Claw."

Surprise rattled through Sara, along with a good dose

of unease. He'd never talked about his years in Vegas, or why he'd left and come to Bear Claw, going straight into the internal affairs department, which was an unusual choice for a transferring cop.

That's old history, she told herself. *It's not important right now.* It meant the drug was working, though. She knew she should steer away from the subject, which wasn't related to the case at hand. But the weak, needy part of herself, the part that had wept for him long after he was gone, needed to know.

"What happened?" she asked softly, figuring that was a general enough question that it didn't entirely violate the trust he'd placed in her when he'd agreed to the pentothal. It came very close, though.

"We were working a series of casino robberies, armored cars being hit on a specific schedule. It was obvious that there were cops involved—payoffs and information being dropped, that sort of thing. We got too close and made the wrong people nervous. A call came in, we answered…it was an ambush. I made it out. She didn't."

The staccato recitation might have robbed the story of its horror if it hadn't been for the grief slashed across his face, the hollowness of his voice.

"Let's focus on—" she started to say, but he wasn't done.

"I didn't realize I loved her until she was gone," he said in a quiet tone that was laced through with self-recrimination. "We never dated, never even kissed. We both knew we couldn't have a relationship like that and stay partners. But eventually we stopped dating other people, too. We joked about our surrogate relationship, not realizing until too late that it was the real thing, at least for me. When she was gone…I lost it. I went after the men who'd set us up, nearly killed two of them, came close to getting myself chucked out of the force for good. But the powers that be were embarrassed by what had been going on under their noses, and let me transfer the hell out of Vegas instead. I couldn't stay there. Not after what had happened. But I couldn't let it go, either."

"So you came to Bear Claw," she said, losing track of the proprieties as things started lining up in her head.

His face smoothed some, though it remained etched with the echoes of grief. "The first week I was in town, I saw you walking from one building to another, wearing a long yellow coat and a wool hat. Pretty, pretty Sara. But I knew you weren't for me. After what happened with Alicia, I didn't want something serious, and you had serious written all over you. Still do."

She knew she should say something, knew she should redirect him to the months after his supposed death, but at the same time she was riveted by what he was telling her. She had a feeling this explained much of what had happened between them, but knew she was still missing pieces of the puzzle. Her moral core said she should stop him, that he'd never given her permission to grill him about his past. But the ex-girlfriend inside her, the one that had always wanted to understand what went wrong between them—that piece of her said to keep going.

Knowing she was better than that, and she owed both

of them more, she said, "The day of the prison riot, you were going there to meet with an informant. Did he have actual information for you, or was that part of the setup for faking your death?"

He frowned. "I don't know. I can't…I can't remember. I remember Alicia, and I remember you. It was that night in the alley, you know. That was the night I ruined everything."

It took her a moment. "You mean when those punk kids hassled us?" She'd all but forgotten about the incident, given what had happened later, when Romo had left the house, supposedly on a call, and had wound up in a bar, going home with another woman. Earlier that night, though, there had been an incident, she remembered now. It had just been another one of those city annoyances to her, but had apparently been more than that to him.

Casting back, she remembered that the night had been dark and rainy, the air heavy with the ominous tingle that presaged thunder and wind. She and Romo had been living together for a few months at that point, and things had been going great—or so she'd thought. They'd been out to dinner with Tucker and Alyssa, Cassie and Seth, and Chelsea and one of the few and fleeting boyfriends she'd had prior to meeting Fax. Sara and Romo had spent the entire meal playing footsie and exchanging caresses under the table, all an unstated warm-up for things to come when they got home. Blood pumping, feeling giddy and foolish with lust and—in her case, at least— love, they'd headed to his car wrapped in each other, oblivious to anything but the prospect of getting naked.

As they'd passed by the mouth of a dark alleyway, shadows had detached themselves from the darkness, two in front, two behind, punks wearing slung-forward hoodies and sneers. Under other circumstances it might've been a really bad situation, but Romo had flashed his badge and gun, and the punks had taken off. She'd been a little surprised that he hadn't detained them while she called for backup, especially knowing that four other cops had just left the restaurant and were close at hand. But that small oddity had soon been lost amid far bigger things, at least to her mind, in the days that followed. Things like infidelity. Like heartbreak. Like the fact that they hadn't gone home and made love; instead, he'd dropped her off and pretended to answer a damned call from his superior at IAD.

"I went back there later," Romo said, pulling her out of her memories and into the moment. "Back to that alley."

He'd opened his eyes and was looking straight at her. Aside from a slight dilation of his pupils, he looked pretty normal. Had the injection worn off so quickly? She didn't know the answer to that any more than she knew why he was suddenly determined to rehash their breakup. But by the same token, she could no more bring herself to stop him now than she'd been able to forgive him back then.

"Why?" she asked softly, beginning to realize there had been far more to that night than she'd ever begun to imagine.

"Because I was furious," he said, his voice all but inflectionless. "Because for a moment, when they were standing around you, making their sleazy threats, I flashed back on what it'd felt like to lose Alicia, and I froze."

Sara frowned. "You didn't freeze. You chased them off by showing them your badge and your gun."

His eyes went cold, reminding her all too strongly of the man he'd been back then. There was zero warmth in his tone when he said, "I didn't go for the gun intending to wave it at them."

"Oh." Blood rushed through her ears, sounding like the ocean. "But—"

"I went back later," he repeated, "because I wanted to teach those guys a lesson. I found two of them, and beat the crap out of them, nearly killed them. I was...I was completely outside myself. Didn't recognize the thing I'd become—all that rage, all that guilt. Until then, I'd been holding it together as our relationship developed. I'd told myself that it was okay, that I could deal with the things I felt for you, because you weren't a cop, weren't likely to find yourself on the wrong end of a gun. But then you did, and I froze. If those punks had been more committed, that night could've ended very, very badly for you."

"That night *did* end very badly for me," she snapped. "Or have you conveniently blocked out the part where you—I'm guessing here, so correct me if I'm wrong—finished your revenge and went straight to the nearest bar, where you bought yourself a couple of shots and a waitress."

He winced and said, "I was all messed up inside my head at that point." It wasn't much of an explanation, but was still more than he'd given her previously regarding the incident. "I'd never told Alicia how I felt—she died not knowing I loved her, with us not ever giving it a chance."

Something went very still inside her. "I'm not Alicia, and you and I were giving our relationship a chance. At least I was. In retrospect, I wonder whether you ever really did." *You never said the words,* she wanted to say, but didn't because that was too weak, too female. She hadn't needed the words—though they would've been nice. What she had needed was fidelity.

"I tried," Romo grated, which wasn't the same as saying that he'd loved her. "But I was starting to struggle even before that night."

She shook her head, baffled. "Struggle with what? I thought we were great together!"

"We were, and that was the problem. The harder I fell, the more terrified I was of losing you. I had nightmares, reliving Alicia's death over and over again, only it wasn't Alicia, it was you."

A half-remembered conversation suddenly clicked into place. "That was why you wanted me to go full-time over at the hospital in the pathology department, rather than sticking with the ME's office."

"I hated that you were anywhere near police work. I wanted to keep you safe, but I knew I couldn't follow you every moment of every day. It wouldn't have been healthy."

"A great deal of this sounds unhealthy," she observed. Leaning forward, she checked his eyes, which looked almost normal. "Is this you or the pentothal talking?" It had to be the drug, she knew. It wasn't as if the real Romo would've voluntarily given up so much of himself, offering her more insight into his inner workings than she'd ever had back when they'd been a couple.

"A combination of the two, I suspect." He rolled his head on his neck, wincing slightly, no doubt when his stitches twinged a protest. "The room's stopped spinning, and I don't feel stoned anymore, but the memories have stuck with me." He paused. "I think I remember everything up to the prison break and the events surrounding it. I've got my parents and my childhood back, which is a huge relief. I've got Vegas and Alicia back, which is far less of a relief, except that it gives me a much better understanding of why, even though we'd broken up, you remained the one person I trusted with my life when I needed help."

"Because you didn't love me as much as you loved Alicia," she said bitterly, finally seeing it after all this time. It wasn't that he'd been fatally flawed as a human being, unable to stay faithful. It had been far worse than that. He had, whether consciously or unconsciously, done the one thing he knew she'd be unable to forgive. He'd wanted out of their relationship, but hadn't had the guts to dump her. Instead, he'd forced her to dump him.

Bastard.

Crossing her arms over her abdomen, where a sharp ache had taken root, she turned partly away from him, wishing she could go to her room and lie down for a few hours. But she'd been the one to drug him. She'd see it through, no matter how badly it hurt.

"You've got it wrong," he said, his voice rough with emotion. "In fact, you've got it entirely backward."

"How's that?" she asked without looking back at him. She didn't want to see the emotion in his face, didn't want to be reminded of the man she'd gotten to know over the past few days, the one who'd accepted his own feelings—and hers—far more readily than the old Romo ever had. He had his memories back; he knew who he was, knew almost everything that mattered. The new Romo was gone, subsumed in the old one, or maybe by the man he'd become over the months he'd been undercover.

But the man he was now—whoever that was— wouldn't let her avoid his eyes. He reached out, pried one of her hands loose from their defensive clench, and clasped her fingers in his. "I sabotaged our relationship because I panicked, pure and simple. I'd started to realize that what I felt for you was ten times stronger than what I'd felt for Alicia. Which meant that the fear of losing you, the terror of having something happen to you, of having to live through that again, was ten times worse, too, if not more." He grimaced and shook his head. "I couldn't…I couldn't be with you, fearing every time you left that you might not come back."

His words tugged at something wistful deep inside her, but she scowled. "So your solution was to sleep with someone else, knowing I'd dump you?"

"It wasn't a solution. It was panic. Only it didn't really fix anything, because even after we broke up I couldn't stop thinking about you, worrying about you. I knew almost immediately that I'd made a huge mistake, but I also knew that it would be a long time— if ever—before you could learn to trust me again. I started seeing a shrink, started trying to fix myself before I tried to fix things with you. Then there was the prison break and the task force, and things went downhill fast."

"You sure picked a strange way to show your affection," she snapped. "Your investigation almost gave Proudfoot the excuse to shut down my office." She tried not to acknowledge that the events of the past few days could very well have sealed that deal for the acting mayor. By now he might know she'd set up the meeting that had nearly killed Fax and Tucker, might even know she was harboring the target of Friday's manhunt. Even if he didn't know those things, there was no way she could show up at work on Monday. She'd be too much of a target.

"My official investigation moved away from the ME's office within the first few days after al-Jihad's prison break," Romo said, his eyes intent on hers, losing the last of their blurriness as she watched.

"Like hell it did. You were breathing down my neck for months after that."

"It was the simplest way to stay close to you and make sure you kept out of the case." His fingers tightened on hers. "When you and the others went off the radar to help Chelsea and Fax that first week after the prison break, I almost lost my mind trying to find you. It…well, let's just say it wasn't pretty." He paused. "I've made mistakes with you, I know that. But I never set out to hurt you. Please believe that, if you believe nothing else about me."

Sara stared at their joined hands for a moment, not sure what she was supposed to say, how she was supposed to feel. One part of her was wearily grateful to finally understand what had gone wrong. Another part wanted to tear at him for pushing her away instead of letting her in on what he was thinking and feeling. And still another part of her—the weak, wanting part—was whispering at the back of her brain, saying that he'd changed, that they might have a chance, after all.

Yeah, rationality said, *just so long as he spends the rest of his life on a low dose of sodium pentothal.* Which so wasn't an option. It was too bad that was what it seemed to take to make him a functional human being.

"My father was a smooth talker," she said slowly, wanting to get the words right and give him the same level of honesty he'd finally given her, drugged or not. "Good apologies aren't enough, though. What I'm looking for— what I deserve—is someone who's willing to be honest within each moment, not after the fact." Forcibly recalling herself to the task at hand, she let go of his hand and reached for the pentothal and another syringe. "Lie back. I'm going to hit you with another dose, see if we can't get you to remember the important stuff."

He sat up, caught the hand that she'd reached toward the drug and once again twined his fingers around hers, hanging on as though he never intended to let go, ever again. "No, don't. I don't think it's a good idea to try again until morning. Besides," he continued before she could argue the point, "I need to tell you something."

She told herself to pull away from him, but couldn't. Instead she looked at him, found herself trapped in his eyes as she whispered, "What?"

The moment the word left her lips she damned herself because she knew—even if he didn't—that she'd just given him permission to break her heart all over again. She hadn't shut him down when she knew she should. Instead, she opened the door a crack.

"I'm not the same man I was," he said, his words ringing with quiet conviction. "I may not know what I've done over the past few months—and trust me, that scares the hell out of me—but I'm sure it involved lots of time alone, probably in that crummy apartment we visited today. Logic says I was cracking code and hacking whatever al-Jihad and the others told me to, but I know from experience that jobs like that involve lots of sitting and thinking."

She told herself she didn't care, that this was just more smooth talk, but couldn't keep from asking, "Thinking about what?"

"Death," he said, which wasn't what she'd expected him to say, and had her jerking her eyes to his in surprise. He smiled grimly, and continued. "And life. I don't remember what I was doing or why, but I guarantee I was thinking how sometimes someone dying is just crappy bad luck, and it doesn't mean the people left behind should stop living."

Emotion balled hard and hot in Sara's throat, but she forced it down, swallowing before she said, "It sounds like being dead was good for you."

He gave a bark of surprised laughter and swung to sit on the edge of the mattress facing her, his knees bumping hers, his face too close, his eyes too intent. "I think it was. The guy you met as he was bleeding all over your living room the other day? That's the man I want to be with you, once all this is over. If you'll give me the chance."

What was she supposed to say to that? She didn't have a clue, knew only that her body was telling her one thing, her head another. And her heart? Well, it had long proven unreliable when it came to Romo, so she didn't figure it should get a vote.

Experience and logic told her that the smart answer was to tell him no, they wouldn't be together ever again. But she couldn't help thinking that he really wasn't the same man she'd known before; she'd recognized it even before he'd made the claim. Whatever he'd done over the past months, whoever he'd become, it had changed him, making him simultaneously more open and more complex, as though his experiences had forced him to accept the part of him that had mourned his dead partner and nearly killed her killers, and later had sent him after the street punks who'd menaced him and Sara in a similar alley.

It was that violence she sensed inside him now, a wildness he hadn't harbored before, or had buried so deeply she hadn't seen it. Somehow in bringing that part of himself to the surface, he'd found the rest of himself, too. She couldn't regret that. But she also wasn't sure she could trust it.

"Please," he said. "Let me make up for everything I did wrong."

Something quivered deep inside her, as she wondered whether he was seeing her as a means to atone for more than just the mistakes he'd made in their relationship. Because of that, because of so many things, she couldn't say yes. She didn't know if she dared try again with him, didn't know if she could trust him going forward. But at the same time she was viscerally aware of the hours passing, of the countdown al-Jihad had imposed on them. It seemed pointless to worry about things that might or might not happen in the future, when she wasn't entirely sure there was going to *be* a future. Yes, she believed that Romo would never willingly allow al-Jihad to harm her—she'd known that even before he'd told her about Alicia, and knowing about his guilt over his dead partner only added another layer of determination. Romo would protect her or die trying. But that was the problem—so far, the terrorist leader had proven untraceable and indefatigable; if he promised to target her, then he would. And he would most likely succeed, unless they somehow managed to outwit his plan. But how were they supposed to do that?

Romo didn't remember what he'd done or who he'd worked for, and he was probably right that she shouldn't repeat the pentothal dosing so soon after the first injection. If she were a trained anesthesiologist, maybe, but she was a pathologist. Keeping her cases alive had never been an option before, much less a priority. She didn't dare take the risk. Which left them—where? They were out of plans, out of ideas. She couldn't contact her friends for fear of endangering their lives more than she already had. Romo couldn't contact his superiors until and unless he remembered who they were, who he could trust.

Despair rose up inside her, threatened to overwhelm her. How was she supposed to think about anything but the danger?

Except that she wasn't thinking entirely about the

danger, was she? Maybe because the situation was so dire, her mind locked on to Romo's plea, his offer. Could there be a future for them? Did it really count as giving him a second chance when he'd changed so thoroughly?

Men don't change; they just say they have, said her inner cynic, who'd learned that lesson early in childhood.

But even though she knew that was true, Sara found that she couldn't bring herself to care about the future just then, didn't really believe she had one. As far as she knew, she had another day or two at the most, and—assuming that they didn't figure out what Romo's mission had been, and use it to bring down al-Jihad—then she'd be headed into protective custody and WitSec relocation at best, a body bag at worst. Most of those options didn't involve her being in Bear Claw beyond the thirty-some hours they had left on their clock, one way or the other.

Given that, logic said they should be focusing on other ways of coming up with Romo's mission and figuring out what information he was supposed to be delivering. Or better, who—if anyone—he could trust within law enforcement, and how he could use that to trap the master terrorist within his own plot. But logic also said they'd tried all the avenues they could for now, that they both needed to rest and recharge. They were as safe as they could make themselves. They needed a break.

And she was rationalizing, she knew. Because, deep down inside, she'd already made her decision.

"No," she said, voice soft because his face was still

very close to her own. "I can't promise to give you another chance once all this is over." She leaned in, closing the distance between them so her words were a breath across his skin as she said, "I will, however, agree to give you the next six hours or so to make your case."

His dark green eyes widened a moment in surprise, then blurred dark, almost black with passion as he closed the final inches between them. His lips brushed against her cheek when he whispered, "Are you sure this is a good idea?"

"Probably not." She reached up and cupped his stubbled jaw in her palms in a gesture that twisted her heart with its awful familiarity, and the brutal heat and longing it brought. "But at this point I don't really care anymore." She blinked hard, and was faintly surprised to feel tears well. "I missed you so damn much," she whispered, her voice breaking.

And even though she knew she was giving in to the weakness and the heat, she couldn't bring herself to care as his lips crushed down on hers in a kiss that washed away indecision and brought with it only heat. Only desire.

Only him.

Chapter Nine

It had been more than a year since the last time Sara and Romo had been together, but those months telescoped to a bad dream at the first touch of his lips, the first soft caress of his tongue against hers. His taste filled her, buoying her with impossible joy that was only slightly tempered by the knowledge that the heat was born of desperation and danger rather than the love and respect she'd once thought they shared. Then even that moment of regret was gone, swept away on a rising tide of need as his lips slanted across hers and his tongue slid along hers in a move that brought a sharp stab of desire deep within her.

The dim light coming from the bathroom lent an air of romance to a room that was anything but romantic. Or maybe the romance was in the moment, in the impossibility that she was once again twining her arms around Romo's neck, that his hands were once again sliding down her body on either side, then up again, cleverly working beneath her shirt to touch skin on skin.

She'd wept at his grave. She'd left flowers, more for

herself than him. It was impossible that she could be touching him again, but his taste was achingly familiar, sharp and edgy, and potently male, like the man himself—Romo the crusader, the warrior. An island unto himself.

Pushing that last thought aside, along with the small, weak part of her that wanted to argue that he really had changed, that he was an entirely different man now, she lost herself in the moment, in the press of his hard, masculine body against hers. She rose against him, twined around him and they eased down to the mattress together.

In deference to the healing wound on his shoulder, they lay on their sides, face-to-face, kissing and touching. Sara's blood spun through her, warm and effervescent as her body shaped against his. She worked her hands beneath his shirt, relearning the warm, yielding flesh she'd touched three days earlier when she'd tended his wounds and marveled at the heat of him.

He groaned, his breath coming fast. Hers was, too, and as they met for another kiss, she felt his excitement as her own. It had been a long time since she'd been with anyone—after a couple of attempts to reenter the dating scene after she and Romo had broken up, she'd turned her attention to her work out of necessity. She didn't ask whether he'd been with anyone in the interim, didn't want to know. And in a way it didn't really matter, because this was the first time for this new—and apparently improved—version of him.

She sensed the differences in him even on the most basic of levels, as he drew his hands along her spine, across her hips and up again to her breasts, where he shaped her most sensitive flesh with gentle, inciting caresses. Pleasure spun through her. She arched against him, rubbed her body along his, wanting to share the powerful sensations. Always before he'd been a thorough, demanding lover. Now, though, he let the moment linger, let the sensations turn soft for a moment before bringing her back to flashpoint with a kiss and a whisper.

She clung to him, shuddering with the enormity of emotions that went way too far within her. All she'd wanted—all she'd been prepared for—was to reconnect with the man she'd loved, and who now claimed he'd cared for her but hadn't known what to do with the feelings, or the fear brought by those emotions. She wasn't ready to open herself to him. Not yet. Maybe not ever again.

Buffering herself against the poignant connection, she turned her face to his and kissed him openmouthed, hard and hot, demanding that he respond in kind. Heat leaped between them, flaring to lust between one heartbeat and the next. He caught her in his arms and held her close, so their bodies shaped one into the other with no gaps, no distance. She could've wept with the mad joy of holding him, and wanted nothing more than to hang on forever, never letting him go.

He's not yours to keep, her inner cynic reminded her, though even that part of her sounded vaguely sad about it.

He paused midkiss and pulled away to look at her with eyes gone dark and serious. He cupped her face in his hands. "Sweet Sara," he said, voice husky with emotion. "I was such a fool."

And there, she realized, was what she'd needed from

him back then. Not the apology, but the owning of what he'd done, what he'd forced her to do in response. And with that acknowledgment, somehow, it was finally, really and truly okay.

Her lips curved and the tears receded, giving way to true pleasure and a sense that she was, for the first time in a long while, exactly where she wanted and needed to be. Yes, terrible danger waited for them beyond the anonymous safety of their hotel room, and there seemed little certainty of success in what they needed to do. But at the same time, somehow, they'd found each other again, had found the connection they'd lost along the way.

Her smile widened. "Hey, Detective," she said, as she'd called him before. "Welcome back."

The creases beside his beautiful eyes deepened and his voice was husky when he said, "It's good to be back."

They left the rest unspoken, because for the moment, just being back was enough for both of them.

After that, she stopped comparing the Romo she was with now with the one she'd loved before. She stopped thinking or planning, stopped analyzing and let herself simply feel. A quick dip into her badly battered handbag yielded the two condoms she carried as much from habit as optimism. She returned to the bed and sank back into Romo, into a kiss that quickly morphed into a hurried race to shed clothing, albeit with some care for his bandages.

His body was lean and tough, roped with capable muscles that slid effortlessly beneath a layer of slick skin and textured with masculine hair. She touched him with her hands, with her mouth, and was surprised to find that they didn't fall back into any sort of rhythm from before. It truly was as though they were coming together for the first time, though with the benefit of some familiarity. She found a new scar along his ribs, another at his hairline, and told herself not to think of where they'd come from, or what he might've done to his attacker. But that fear added poignancy to their next kiss, and brought a sharp edge to the pleasure as he touched her with clever, inciting fingers, bringing her to a point hovering at the edge of madness and keeping her there as they twined together, bound by need and remembered loneliness.

In that moment there was no past or future, there was only sensation. The world coalesced to the feel of skin on skin, the taste of him on her lips and tongue, the sound of his harsh groans, his voice whispering praise and pleasure. Foil ripped and he dealt with the condom, then returned to her, touching her once again, bringing her up until need coiled hard and hot and joining with him was as necessary as her next breath.

"Romo," she said in invitation, in demand. It wasn't a plea, though. She was done asking.

She arched against him, heard him catch his breath as he shifted, rose above her and paused a moment, poised to join his hard length to her body.

"Sara," he said, and stayed motionless until she opened her eyes. She found herself trapped in the openness of his expression, the intensity and unexpected tenderness when he said, "If you remember nothing else about me, remember this—you've been in my heart all along, even when I was too stubborn, too scared to admit it."

Tears skimmed along the surface of her soul, adding an aching sweetness to the moment when he shifted and slipped inside her. There was a pang of resistance, a stiffness of muscles long unused; then there was nothing but the feeling of him, of the two of them together. He filled her, surrounded her. Completed her, though she'd always hated the word, and the concept. She was fully complete on her own. But she was more than that when she was with him, she knew, and damned herself for the knowledge.

Twining her arms around his shoulders and turning her face into his neck as he thrust home, she told herself that it was just for tonight, no future or past, no expectations. If she expected nothing, she couldn't get hurt again, right? Then her body started moving in time with his, in a rhythm as ancient, natural and life-giving as the act of breathing, and she wasn't thinking anymore. She was feeling.

They surged together and apart, together and apart, loving each other without calling it love. The tempo increased from a slow wave to a slap of flesh on flesh, a building burn of intensity. Sara closed her eyes and pressed her cheek to his, giving herself over to the moment, to the man. Heat spiraled within her, took her over. She burrowed into him, clung to him, shuddered with him as they chased each other over the edge into madness.

The orgasm gripped her in a wave of sharp-edged pleasure, stealing her breath and her thoughts. She bowed back, crying his name as he cut loose within her and came, shuddering in her arms.

Pleasure suffused her, took her over, held her motionless for an eternal moment that ended far too soon. Because once it ended, once the madness dimmed and reality returned, she found herself wrapped around Romo, clinging to him as though he were the only solid object in the universe they'd found themselves in. She might as well cling to quicksilver, she knew, because he wouldn't stay put, wouldn't be tamed, no matter what he said about being a new, improved version of himself.

But even as she thought that, she couldn't help the wistful wondering of *what if?* What if he'd truly changed? What if they made it through the next few days somehow? What if there actually could be a future for the two of them, a second chance that wasn't really a second chance?

"Hush," he said, kissing her brow.

She frowned up at him. "I didn't say anything."

His lips quirked upward in a smile. "You're thinking very loudly."

That startled a laugh out of her. "Sorry to disturb you."

"No problem. But do me a favor and don't overthink it quite yet, okay? Tomorrow will be here soon enough." There was a trace of sadness in his words, as though he, too, recognized that they were out of options and plans, that there didn't seem to be a next strategy to try.

He shifted to his side, and slid from the bed to use the bathroom. When he returned, he slipped in beside her and gathered her close, fitting them together back to front. Looping an arm around her, he linked their fingers over her heart and simply held her as the hotel quieted around them and night took hold.

They dozed for a bit, ordered room service near midnight, made love again and then slept, exhausted. Sara dreamed of him as she hadn't done since the funeral, which had put a final end—or so she'd thought—to any prospect of them being together ever again. She woke early, just as the sun was starting to lighten the world beyond the window. The dim light showed her his stern profile, gone soft at the edges in postcoital sleep.

He slept sprawled on his stomach, with his face smashed into the soft hotel pillow and one of his hands loosely holding one of her wrists, touching her in sleep as though he feared she might disappear on him.

How many times had she watched him like this, and wondered what he was dreaming? Always before, she'd known he had secrets that drove him, corralled him. Now, knowing about what had happened to him in Vegas, she thought she understood better why he'd had a hard time accepting that he'd fallen for her, and that their relationship should follow the more or less natural progression from dating to lovemaking, to nights spent at each other's places, to living together.

In retrospect, she was almost surprised they'd gotten that far. Him moving into her house had been his idea, one that had seemed more than reasonable given that they spent most nights there together anyway. It had, again, seemed more than reasonable for him to keep his own apartment for six months or so, in case it didn't work out, or it turned out they needed more space than offered by her little house. At the time it had all seemed perfectly logical. Now she realized it had been more of a test than she'd realized at the time. He'd been challenging himself, experimenting to see whether he could live with her and still hold a piece of himself apart.

It'd be different for us this time, she thought, though the words rang hollow inside her own skull. That hollowness weighed on her, prompting her to lean in and touch her lips to his, waking him with a kiss.

His lips curved under hers and he kissed her back thoroughly, wonderfully. Humming her pleasure, she moved into him, but he didn't take it further, instead easing away to look at her, his green eyes serious and searching. "Morning," he said, but what she thought he meant was, *Do you regret last night?*

"Morning," she returned, and let the warmth in her soul turn her lips up in a smile that she hoped answered his questions.

Instead of easing, his expression grew darker. He sat up, pulling the sheet with him to pool in his lap. "Sara, we need to talk, and you're not going to like what I have to tell you."

Something froze inside her. Fear flared. *Oh, God. What now?* Whatever it was, she could see from his face that it was serious, and very bad.

Feeling suddenly too naked and vulnerable, she slipped from the bed, taking the comforter with her as a shield. "Let me get dressed." She grabbed her clothes and escaped to the bathroom, where she glared at herself in the mirror. "Don't," she said harshly, "be an idiot." That was the only pep talk she could come up with, because she didn't know what was coming next. It might be some sort of dangerous plan she wouldn't like—at this point she almost hoped it was, because the alternative was something along the lines of "it's not you, it's me."

Grimly determined not to lose her cool, she washed her face and brushed her teeth with the toiletries they'd had sent up with their room service meal. She heard Romo's voice out in the other room, and assumed he was ordering breakfast, or at the very least, coffee. Neither of them was at their best before caffeine in the morning. By the time she returned to the main room, he was dressed once again, and had pulled the bed to rights, albeit without the comforter she'd dragged into the bathroom.

Trying not to feel as though he'd tried to erase the evidence of their lovemaking from the hotel room, she returned the comforter to the bed and sat cross-legged at the foot of the mattress, facing him. "Did I hear you calling down for breakfast?"

"Among other things," he said cryptically. "Coffee and bagels will be up in a few minutes."

"And after that?" she said, figuring there was nothing to be gained by delaying.

"I don't need more pentothal," he said simply.

It took a moment for the words to penetrate, another for her to grasp their meaning. "You remember the rest of it now?" Maybe sleep had helped his brain sort out the flashes. She had the sinking feeling that wasn't what he was saying, though.

He shook his head, grimacing. "Not just now. I remembered it all right away." He paused, and then said harshly, "I lied when I told you I didn't remember anything past the prison break. I had all of it, right up here." He tapped his temple, as though daring her to respond.

She would have, but she didn't know how. "What…" She trailed off, brain spinning, and was saved from continuing to flounder when a knock at the door announced the arrival of their coffee and bagels.

Her appetite was gone, but she went for the coffee while Romo tipped the hotel staffer for the delivery. Loaded with cream and sugar, the coffee warmed her where she'd gone cold, steadied her where she'd gone unsteady. Her body vibrated with confusion and the hollow hurt of betrayal, but over all that was a stinging sense of self-disgust that she'd left herself open for his apparent lies and betrayal by doing exactly what she'd promised herself time and again that she *wouldn't* do.

Yes, Romo had lied to her; yes, he'd betrayed her. But she'd given him the opportunity and power by letting him back into her heart when she knew better, damn it.

When they were alone again, she returned to her seat on the bed and wrapped her chilled fingers around her mug of coffee. Romo took his own coffee and leaned against the bureau. His eyes never left hers as he lifted his mug and sipped, waiting for her response, braced for the fight, for the recriminations and the blast of her fury.

"I'm not going to yell at you, or get hysterical, or cry and accuse you of being all the things you already know you are," she said finally, feeling a wave of weariness that cut through her to her bones, chasing away the warmth she'd so recently felt in his arms. "Why bother? It didn't seem to make an impact one way or the other the last time, and this time is no different."

Something flashed in his eyes, and he moved as if to set the coffee aside and cross to her, but stopped himself and stayed put. His voice, though, grated with raw intensity when he said, "This time is entirely different. *I'm* different."

"Not from where I sit," she said. When he would've argued, she raised a hand to stop him. "Please. Let's not do this. There are more important things to deal with than who said what, or who did or didn't do the right thing." She paused, waiting for his shallow, tight-lipped nod before she said, "Tell me everything." Which, she suspected, wouldn't actually be everything. Instead, it would be what he chose to share with her. As usual.

"You were right from the very beginning," he said, as though that should matter to her at this point. "I can't tell you all of it, for both our sakes, but suffice it to say that when I was contacted by what I thought could be an arm of al-Jihad's network, looking for a programmer with federal database experience and an expensive lifestyle, I played along while contacting someone we both trust higher up in the task force. He put me in touch with the right people, and we cobbled together a plan to put me undercover. Al-Jihad's people faked my death and set me up in that crummy apartment, with a fat offshore account and all the computer power I could want. I hacked into the accounts they told me to, cracked the codes they needed, always just seeing little pieces of the puzzle, never the whole." He paused and fixed her with a look. "And like I said, I had lots of time alone to think about where I'd gone wrong in my life."

Sara shook her head. "I can't care about that anymore." She knew she should feel vindicated to learn that she'd been right about him, knew she should probably be proud of him for sacrificing his life and his freedom in an effort to bring peace back to Bear Claw. All she could find inside her was emptiness, though. "What was the mission?"

"My federal contact wanted me to find a missing USB key that Lee Mawadi had hidden in a ceramic statue belonging to his wife, Mariah. She had divorced him while he was in prison, but the statue was her mother's, and had enough sentimental value that he figured she'd keep it with her. Shortly before the prison riot, the task force became aware of the existence of this flash drive, and that the statue had been returned to Mariah's mother. The FBI almost retrieved it in time, but Mawadi got to one of the drivers, nearly got to Mariah, too. She survived, thanks to her FBI protector, Grayson, but al-Jihad's people had the flash drive. That was right about when I was first contacted, so the thought—the hope—was that they'd called me in to work on whatever information was contained on the drive. We figured my first few assignments were more tests than anything, so I played them straight, trying to work my way into the terrorists' confidence."

Sara's stomach soured on the image of Romo sitting alone in that depressing apartment, working for the terrorists. He would've been in fear for his life every moment of every day. Technically he'd already been dead, at least as far as the rest of the world had been concerned. One misstep, one mistake, and the terrorists could have killed him and hidden his body, and only a few people would've known anything had gone wrong. From what little she'd learned of Fax's undercover experiences—and she had to assume Fax was the "mutual friend" Romo had gone to for his undercover contact— the covert agency he'd worked for was quick to cut its losses, and was as compartmentalized as the terrorist networks it targeted, meaning that help and trust were often rare commodities.

She thought about how he must have lived, and instinctively knew it'd been worse than she could probably imagine. "What happened in the end?" she asked dully.

"I earned the trust I needed, and got called to meet a couple of guys on one of the state forest access roads. They brought me to a cabin, handed me a laptop and ordered me to break the encryption on a group of files that dated back to when Mawadi hid the flash drive. I cracked the code, waited until they weren't paying attention and copied the files to my own flash. I erased the hell out of my tracks, but somehow I tripped up and they figured out I was working for the other side." He grimaced. "Either that, or my work was done and they had decided I was expendable. Regardless, it became clear real quick that they didn't intend to bring me back to my truck." He lifted a hand to his healing shoulder. "I fought them off, killed one and went after the other. I'd warned my contact where I was going, so when I got the Mayday out, he had a team after me almost immediately. Unfortunately—and this is where it's still a little fuzzy—I took the bullet and the blow to the head, and lost track of who I could trust." The look he sent her said, *Except I knew I could trust you.*

She couldn't let that matter, though. Not anymore. "Where's the flash drive?"

"Hidden in my shoe." His lips twitched. "An oldie but goodie."

She glanced at the battered boots he'd retrieved from her gun cabinet that first night, and sighed. "So what now?" She knew she should be relieved to know they weren't on their own anymore, that he knew who he could call for help, that maybe they would be able to deal with al-Jihad's threat, after all. But the realization did little to improve the hollow, empty feeling that came from knowing that Romo hadn't changed at all. He'd lied to her. Again, and for the last time.

"I called in already." Romo glanced out the window. "There are cars on the way, one to bring me in, the other carrying a couple of guys who'll take you someplace safe while we get this taken care of."

He might've couched it all in very vague terms, but she got the gist that she was to be locked away under protective custody while the covert group, using the information encrypted on Romo's flash drive, tried to bring down the terrorist mastermind once and for all.

A week ago, she would've jumped at the chance to disappear from the dangerous situation. She was a pathologist, not a cop, an agent or a spy. She had liked her life simple and even-keeled, and had wanted more than anything for al-Jihad to be recaptured and life in Bear Claw to return to normal, including plans for the special election that would—she devoutly hoped—replace Percy Proudfoot with a somewhat more forward-thinking mayor.

Now, though, she found herself resisting the idea of passivity. She wanted to go with Romo, wanted to understand how he could walk away from his life with no guarantee of safety or success.

He'd said he'd lusted after her from afar, that he'd gone into counseling, hoping that they could start over. But how did that mesh with his decision to go undercover? How did a man who wanted a future throw his present away and let the woman he supposedly loved think he was dead?

He'd been watching her process all the new information, and must have seen something of that confusion on her face, because he crossed to her and touched her cheek. "This terrorist thing is bigger than the two of us, Sara. It's bigger even than Bear Claw. I didn't have a choice. Al-Jihad doesn't make many mistakes, but he did with me. I had to take advantage of that. I hope you can understand that, and forgive me."

His words and the fleeting caress left sparks behind, making her want to snap at him because of the way he could make her body respond, despite everything that kept happening between them. But because her body's response was her problem, not his, and because he was right about the terror threat being more important than individual lives at this point, she held in her frustration.

Just because she understood, though, didn't mean she had to forget. She lifted her chin and looked him in the eye. "I can forgive you for dying on me. But I can't see that there's any excuse for you not telling me all of this until just now. You should've told me last night."

He looked away. "I wanted to tell you how I felt without the other stuff overshadowing what I needed to say."

"Baloney," she said, sick at heart because she saw the lie for what it was. "You wanted to get laid."

His eyes went very hard, and it was entirely the old Romo who said, "That's ugly."

"Truth hurts."

"Especially when it's your version of the truth." His voice was as cold as his expression, though she thought she saw a layer of hurt beneath.

"There's no such thing as different versions of the truth," she retorted. "It's either true or it isn't."

He gritted his teeth, looking furious, but his voice was somehow soft and sad when he said, "I was miserable without you, Sara, and crazy with it. I was just starting to get less crazy when this undercover thing came up, but instead of making me more crazy, somehow it simplified things for me. I want to be with you," he said, while emotion froze her in place and stole the voice from her throat. He continued. "But I'm not perfect. I want you, and when this garbage is over I want to try to make a life with you. But I can't tiptoe on eggshells, trying not to make mistakes and trigger your no-second-chances button. You're going to have to learn to accept an apology and move on, or this can't go anywhere."

The sense of hope that had tried to flare died beneath a wash of cool reality. She rose from the bed, moving past him. "I assume your reinforcements are waiting for us downstairs?"

His eyes blanked. "They should be."

"And you're sure you can trust the men in this group?"

"Fax does," he said, as if he instinctively understood that she'd take her friend's word over his own at this point.

She nodded. "Let's go."

But he blocked her at the doorway, the chill in his expression losing way to cold fury and hot, spiky frustration. "That's it? That's all I get from you?"

"You want more?" She drilled a finger into his chest, forced herself not to let the touch linger. "Fine, here goes. Fundamentally, people don't change. I've always known that, and I've always applied the knowledge to choosing the people I care for. But you know what? It applies the other way around, too. You're asking me to accept that you are who you are. I can respect that, but I don't think I can do it, because you're asking me to change something that's fundamental to me. You don't like my take on no second chances? Well then, tell me where it stops."

She gestured around the room, encompassing the two of them, and their shared history. "I'm supposed to forgive you for cheating on me, because you were scared, and because you were dealing with some baggage that you've gotten some counseling for. Okay, so say I forgive you for that one. But after that you practically stalked me in my office, endangering my job just because you wanted an excuse to be near me." She ticked off the points on her fingers. "Then you fake your own death and disappear on me for half a year. After that, you come to me, endanger my life, put my friends' lives at risk, tear me away from my work and my home…and when you finally have an opportunity to come clean, you don't. You tell me just enough to make me want to be with you again, saving the rest for the morning after." She broke off, breathing hard, as though she'd been running for her life instead of listing off his sins. "So you tell me. Where does the flexibility stop and the truth begin?"

Romo's eyes had gone hooded during her recitation, his face set in stone. At her question, he dipped his head so they were eye level when he said, "It begins with faith. And you have none."

Without another word he turned and yanked open the door, and all but hauled her downstairs. He handed her off to her new guards—two stone-faced men in gray suits who could've been bookends for each other— and slammed into the second car without looking back.

Sara climbed into the dark SUV her guards had arrived in, and held herself stiff and still as they pulled away from the hotel, headed for a safe house.

For the first few miles, she saw nothing but Romo's face, heard nothing but his voice. After a while, though, she put that aside, realizing none of it had an answer. Looking around herself, she saw that she was separated from the driver and his buddy by a layer of dark, tinted glass. There were no lock releases on the doors, no button to buzz down the partition, suggesting she was riding in what might normally serve for prisoner trans-port. The realization brought a flash of unease, quickly swept away when she remembered what Romo had said about Fax trusting the people she was with. That was good enough for her. It was going to have to be.

"See? I have faith," she said to the lingering memory of Romo's accusations.

Numbly, she watched the scenery pass her windows, as the suburbs went to forest and the road began to climb. It wasn't until the vehicle turned onto an access road and stopped beside a low-slung sedan that her nerves started to flare. She reached to fumble for her purse, only then realizing that one of the guards had taken her bag when he'd helped her into the SUV. He must have the purse—and the .22—in the front.

Panic threatened. However, when a tall, elegant, professionally dressed woman emerged from the sedan, Sara relaxed and blew out a breath, telling herself not to freak out. They were just picking up another agent, this one a woman. Her sex shouldn't have mattered, but Sara thought she'd rather not be surrounded entirely by men for a while. They were getting on her nerves.

The woman opened the far door of the SUV and climbed into the compartment where Sara sat. The driver stood behind her, glowering, all but daring Sara to try to make a break for it. But he probably looked at all his protectees that way, she reassured herself as the woman slid in beside her and nodded for the driver to lock them in.

"Are you another of my guards?" Sara asked as the SUV got under way again, heading deeper into the woods.

The woman nodded, her lips tipping up slightly. "You could say that."

"I'm Sara."

The other woman hesitated, then held out a hand.

"It's a pleasure to finally meet you, Dr. Whitney. You can call me Jane Doe."

Sara's relief morphed to panic in an instant as she recognized the name of Fax's former boss, the one who'd put him undercover in the ARX Supermax Prison and later proved to be working on collusion with al-Jihad himself. Terror spiked adrenaline into Sara's bloodstream and she reacted instantly, hurling herself at the window beside her. It gave slightly but didn't crack. She was trapped!

She didn't scream because nobody there would care that she was afraid. Instead, gritting her teeth, she lunged up on the seat and kicked at the window, cursing and spitting.

"Relax," Jane said, and Sara felt a prick on her right butt cheek. An injection!

Now she did scream, and she lashed out a kick at the double agent. But the kick didn't land. Instead, her legs went to water and she slumped down as the drug Jane had injected her with took hold and the world went gray.

"Help me," Sara slurred as she collapsed and unconsciousness closed in, leaving her last few words to echo only in her skull. *Romo, damn it. Where are you when I need you?*

But the answer was obvious, wasn't it? He was gone, because she'd told him to go. There were no second chances in her world.

Chapter Ten

When the dark SUV pulled up to the curb midcity, Romo recognized the building in the heart of Bear Claw, though he'd only been there once before. The average passerby never would've guessed the space had been taken over by a covert ops group so secret it didn't even really have a name. The building was squat and rectangular, stuck amid several similar buildings, with nothing much to recommend it aside from its relative anonymity.

But M. K. O'Reilly and the other members of the Cell preferred it that way. Anonymous was effective, in their line of work.

Flanked on either side by his driver and another agent, both fully armed and silent, Romo headed for the boss's office, aware that his escorts would shoot him without a qualm if it looked for a second as if he posed a threat. Mission or no mission, nobody trusted an undercover agent fresh in from the field.

Well, that was fine with him; he didn't intend to pose a threat to anyone except al-Jihad and his people. He wanted to get this over with, so he could… Hell, he thought, frustration and anger combining inside him, forming a hard knot in his gut, he didn't know what he was going to do next, but he knew he damn well didn't want to do it in Bear Claw. He was done with the city, done with trying to make things work for him there.

He'd left Vegas for Colorado to forget Alicia and the mistakes he'd made with her. He had a feeling he was going to have to go farther than a state or two away before he started to forget Sara.

Damn it, he wasn't blameless in their issues, it was true. But he couldn't do all the work, either. She was going to have to meet him partway. Or rather, she would have to meet him if she had any desire to make it work. She'd said she loved him, back then. But he was starting to think she'd loved him only when it hadn't been complicated for her, when it hadn't challenged some of the rules she'd set for herself long ago.

"In here." One of Romo's heretofore silent escorts waved him through an office door, interrupting his inner frustration with Sara's intransigence, and his own inability to just walk the hell away from her.

The name on the door was M. K. O'Reilly, with no rank or position listed. But then again, nobody who got this far inside the building needed O'Reilly's status spelled out. He was, quite simply, the boss. The fixer.

O'Reilly was a no-nonsense career agent in his midfifties with thirty years on the job and an unimpeachable record. He'd taken over the nameless covert ops group formerly headed by Jane Doe, and had immediately set about bringing them partway into the light.

Where before the group had been off the books, funded through a shell within a shell, out of discretionary funds leeched off several other groups within the CIA and FBI, now it was an official covert ops group called the Cell. The Cell was still organized as it had been under Jane Doe's leadership, with the main operatives working independently of one another, often tasked with specific projects without knowledge of the larger whole, much as al-Jihad's dispersed network was arranged. However, under O'Reilly's leadership, the operatives each interfaced with two senior agents in addition to the boss, so as to avoid—in theory, anyway— the isolation that had led to Fax being put deep undercover, unknowingly working on behalf of the terrorists when Jane Doe had turned traitor.

The reorganization, however, didn't mean the Cell was warm and fuzzy, by any means. The building— dubbed the Cell Block, both as a nod to the group's new name and because of its austere nondécor—was a spartan setup intended more for function than comfort. O'Reilly's office was a plain room decorated with basic furniture, a high-powered laptop, and drifts of papers, photos and printouts. Much like the office, O'Reilly himself was spare and functional looking, and a little disheveled in a dark suit and striped tie. His salt-and-pepper hair was neatly trimmed, but stood on end as though he'd run his hands through it in frustration one too many times. His careworn face was set in dour folds that lightened fractionally when Romo strode through the door.

"Damn good to see you alive, Detective."

"Technically, I'm not," Romo said dryly, but shook

hands with his erstwhile boss. "Sorry I got delayed." He'd sketched out the situation when he'd phoned in, hitting the high points while glossing over a few details—such as how he'd finally regained his memory, and what he'd done in the aftermath of the pentothal dosing. At the time, making love to Sara had seemed like an excellent idea. Now, fully sober, he had to admit it hadn't been one of his better moves.

Undoubtedly taking Romo's grimace as pertaining to his bout with amnesia, O'Reilly said, "Understood, but you're here now. Let's see what you've brought us." He waved Romo to the desk, with its powerful laptop. "Did you get a look at the file's contents when you were decrypting the flash?"

"Just a glance," Romo answered as he snagged O'Reilly's chair, slipped off one of his battered boots and retrieved the flash from the deceptively simple hiding spot he'd hollowed out, hidden beneath the sweat-stained lining and Odor-Eaters he'd installed to dissuade casual searchers from groping around in the boots. Fitting the flash into the USB port on the side of O'Reilly's computer, he said, "It looked like a detailed schematic of the ARX Supermax Prison, which stands to reason given that al-Jihad, Mawadi and Feyd all broke out. They would've had to explore a bunch of options before deciding on using Jane Doe to put Fax in place with instructions to help them escape. Except for one thing." Romo flicked a glance at O'Reilly.

The senior agent muttered a curse, seeing the problem. "Mawadi hid the flash drive before he was arrested for the Santa Bombings."

"Which would suggest they expected—or had planned—to be incarcerated in the ARX Supermax," Romo said as he pulled up the files and started the decryption chain he'd worked out right before al-Jihad's thugs had attacked him in the forest cabin, trying—and failing—to tie up the loose ends. *Well,* he thought, *if I have anything to say about it, this loose end is going to be the key to unraveling this whole mess.* Which was an optimistic thought, granted, but he figured he could use some damned optimism right about then.

For a moment, the thought of personally helping to bring down al-Jihad sent a thrill of anticipated victory through Romo's bloodstream, muting his frustration with how other things were going in his life. Or the life he meant to reclaim as soon as all this was over. Still, though, there was a small kernel of sadness at the back of his brain, one that said he might not come out the winner in all things. In the end, he might not win Sara, despite having done the best he'd known how, under the circumstances.

Yes, he hadn't been fully honest with her, but his secrets had been on the level of national security. Surely she could see the difference there? He shook his head, telling himself she was being unreasonable, telling himself to ignore the buzzing suspicion that she hadn't been wrong about all of it, that he was still missing something.

"If they were researching the prison even before the bombing, then this entire thing has been part of one overarching plan." O'Reilly leaned over Romo's shoulder. "Yeah, that looks like the ARX, all right. But if that's the case, then his message to you doesn't make any sense. He's already out, and he's got his own copy of the plans. Why would he care about having you return this one?"

"There's another file." Romo pulled it up, showed his boss a second set of schematics. "It's a tunnel system of some sort—maybe mine shafts? I don't know where they start or end, though."

There was dead silence from O'Reilly.

Romo looked over his shoulder, and decided he didn't like the look on the senior agent's face one bit. "What is it? You recognize the second map?"

"I sure do," O'Reilly growled. "Except there's a tunnel that shouldn't be there." He pointed to a long, straight line that started at the very edge of the clustered shafts, and headed due west.

A cold chill shimmered down Romo's spine. "Don't tell me. This mess is east of the prison."

"Okay. I won't tell you."

Romo ignored that and paused, frowning. "But why the hell would they want to get themselves tossed in the jail, go to the trouble of escaping, but then, what? Try to break back in?"

"They must've needed to set up something on the inside," O'Reilly muttered. "Something al-Jihad himself had to oversee."

Romo sent him a sardonic look. "This can't be the first time the possibility has come up."

The senior agent's expression went shuttered. "There are a million theories, any hundred of which could fit the evidence, depending on the details."

In other words, O'Reilly wasn't sure how far he trusted Romo, who was a newcomer to the Cell, lacked federal training and had been undercover for most of the time he'd been affiliated with the group. Rather than taking offense, Romo nodded. "Understood."

O'Reilly's expression flattened and the men stared at each other for a long moment before the senior agent sighed heavily. "Oh, what the hell. We're at a standstill here. Maybe you'll see something we've missed." He nudged Romo aside and called up a trio of files onto the computer screen. "These are encoded—maybe encrypted?—transmissions we've intercepted over the past week. The chatter says something big is coming down the pipeline, and thanks to the intel you just brought, we can guess where it's going to happen, but we need more than that before we can move. We're pretty sure al-Jihad is planning a massive jailbreak, partly as an outright terror attack on the region, partly as a means to release a number of key operatives from other major terror groups. Some of the rumors suggest that he's looking to centralize all the major anti-American groups, with the aim of striking a fatal blow against the country as a whole. If he gets the political prisoners free, earning their loyalty—or at least putting them in his debt—well, what happens next will make the Santa Bombings look like a warm-up act." The senior agent sighed heavily, the prospect cutting deep grooves in the tired lines of his face. "We need a timeline, and details. Al-Jihad is smart. Too smart. There's no way he doesn't have backup plans within backup plans. Take a look at the transmissions, will you? Maybe you'll see something we missed."

Romo swallowed heavily, appalled by the picture O'Reilly had painted. "T'll see what I can do." He glanced up at the senior agent. "You want me out of your office?"

"No. Stay. That computer is a closed system, not networked to anything. It's as safe as you're going to get."

"Gotcha." But the mention of safety brought up the specter that hovered far too near Romo's conscious mind at all times these days—the safety of the people in Bear Claw who had become so important to him. "How are Fairfax and McDermott doing?" he asked, guilt stabbing as he realized he hadn't yet asked, when he'd been at least practically responsible for their injuries. Amnesia or not, he should've been smarter about setting up the meeting, more careful about the peripherals.

"McDermott is on the mend. Fax was discharged yesterday, though he'll be on restricted duty until those ribs heal." A faint smile touched O'Reilly's lips. "I gather his fiancée is sticking him with the remainder of the wedding planning while she finishes her training."

Romo snorted appreciatively at the image that brought, of petite, dynamo Chelsea turning into a superagent, while Fax—who already was a superagent— ordered flowers and sorted RSVPs. In the craziness of the situation, Romo was only just beginning to realize how much more than just himself he'd regained when he'd gotten his memory back.

"Any word from Sara's detail?" he asked next, knowing they both knew she was really the one he wanted to know about.

He couldn't get past the look she'd had on her face as he'd told her the truth about his memory. He'd made a judgment call in not telling her right away that he'd regained all of his memory, and even after the fallout, he still thought he'd done the right thing. True, if he'd copped to the other memories right away, he could've returned to the Cell a few hours earlier. But he'd wanted—needed—that time for himself, damn it. He'd needed it for them, as a chance to tell her all the things he'd wanted to tell her months earlier, but had instinctively known she wasn't ready to hear. He hoped to hell when all this was over she could forgive him for it, that she could find a way to understand and be flexible.

Unfortunately, that thought bumped up against the fear that she wouldn't be able to find that flexibility, or that he'd damaged their relationship so deeply she wouldn't want to try.

"The agents with her checked in on schedule," O'Reilly said, voice faintly dismissive, as though protective custody of a single medical examiner was the least of his worries. Which it probably was. For Romo, though, it was a primary concern.

Making love to her the night before had been incredible. It had been healing. Cleansing. A homecoming. But at the same time, his timing had been off. If he'd been fully in control of himself, he probably would have waited. Then again, he acknowledged inwardly, maybe not, because there was no guarantee that there would be a tomorrow for either of them. Not unless he and the others made some major breakthroughs, fast.

"I'll get to work on this," he said, nodding to the information on the computer screen.

"I'll lock you in," O'Reilly said on his way out, and suited action to words.

Months ago Romo would've taken offense at the show of caution, becoming angry that he'd walked away from his life, sacrificing himself in the name of justice without gaining the trust that sacrifice should imply. Months ago, he'd been an idiot, he admitted inwardly as his fingers flew over the keyboard in familiar patterns, beginning the decryption process. Or if not a complete idiot, at least far too caught up in his own wants and needs, his own bruised ego and what he perceived himself as being owed. Being dead had taught him a few things, not the least of which was that there were times and places where the individual didn't—couldn't—matter.

When he'd been a kid, watching his family nearly fall apart under the strain of the false accusations against his father, he'd been dimly aware of the larger scope of things, and how the ripple effect of the embezzlement had hurt families beyond his own. But his parents, their lawyers and the cops who'd eventually cracked the case and arrested his father's partner instead…they had all focused on the small stuff, the little details. They'd had to—that had been the nature of the case.

That had been true for most of the cases Romo had investigated throughout his career, too. He and Alicia had worked at the local level, albeit on the high-dollar scale intrinsic to Vegas. Even the corruption they'd stumbled on had been very personal—a handful of dirty cops and two very powerful moneymen. After her death, he'd run from his grief—he was willing to admit now that he'd run rather than dealing, rather than healing. He'd wound up in Bear Claw working internal affairs, which had suited his need for justice while staying on the small, familiar scale. Then al-Jihad had escaped from the ARX Supermax, and that small, familiar scale had widened abruptly.

At the time he'd thought he'd been doing everything right, bearing down on the hints of local-level corruption and conspiracy because that was what he knew how to do, and because it freed the federal agents to do the bigger-picture stuff. But over time he'd realized this wasn't the sort of case that could be deconstructed to the smaller scale, not really. In leading a witch hunt in his own PD, he'd taken attention away from where it needed to be—higher up the food chain.

Which, he realized as he came up against a dead end in his decryption, backed up and tried a different route, wasn't unlike what he'd done with Sara. He'd accused her of being intransigent, and dared her to give him another chance. As with making love to her under only partial honesty, the challenge had seemed like a good idea at the time, but as he worked on the encrypted transmissions, he started to wonder whether that hadn't been another misstep on his part. He had, whether he'd intended to or not, asked her to give him a pure pass on one of her most fundamental beliefs—that of fidelity.

Yes, he'd apologized for what he'd done, and he'd explained the situation, at least partly. But he'd never really admitted he'd been wrong to do it. And he'd never promised not to do it again. Without those assurances, how was it fair to put the fault back on her?

"Damn," he muttered under his breath. "I *am* an idiot." However, on the plus side, it'd only taken him a few hours to realize it this time, rather than the weeks or months he'd gone previously. Surely that was evidence against her belief that people couldn't change?

He should call the safe house and—

His fingers paused as his eyes locked on a piece of code. One part of him had been hard at work while his heart thought of Sara, and damned if he didn't think he'd found what the other analysts had missed. Maybe he'd seen it because he'd looked at so many other of the terrorists' files, maybe because he hadn't been trained in the FBI program, who knew? What mattered was that he was pretty sure he could break the damn thing.

Focusing, setting aside his other thoughts and worries, he got down to the serious business of decrypting. When O'Reilly checked on him fifteen minutes later, he was halfway there. The senior agent left the door unlocked when he ducked back out, and coffee appeared at Romo's elbow a few minutes later.

Something unknotted inside him—a tightness he'd been carrying for so long now, he hadn't really been aware of it until it was gone, banished by the feeling of finally having come in from the cold, finally being a part of something larger than his small, angry world.

Just under an hour from when he'd entered O'Reilly's office, Romo pushed away from the computer with a sound of satisfaction. "Gotcha, you bastards." His satisfaction, though, was badly tainted with dismay, because the information he'd uncovered meant that they didn't have much time to counter al-Jihad's nefarious plan.

O'Reilly appeared in the doorway, though Romo hadn't been aware of the senior agent hovering. More than likely, he'd tasked an underling to keep an eye on Romo's progress and signal him when it looked as though things were getting ready to break free. "Tell me something good," O'Reilly demanded.

"I can tell you something, all right."

"But not good."

"Not so much." Romo waved the senior agent forward, so they were both looking at the screen. After a quick rundown of the methods he'd used to crack the encryption, he summarized, "It's a set of instructions to Weberly."

"Damn it." A muscle pulsed alongside O'Reilly's square jaw at the news. Weberly was the new head warden of the ARX Supermax, having been promoted into the position following his predecessor's death during the prison riot. "The riot wasn't just designed to cover your death," O'Reilly growled.

Romo shook his head. "I think that was a side benefit. The main goal was clearing the way for Weberly. Hell, for all we know, that was why al-Jihad, Feyd and Mawadi orchestrated their arrest and incarceration, as a means to develop the most useful contacts inside the prison." He grimaced. "It houses the worst of the worst, which is why the terrorists targeted it. Al-Jihad and the others wanted to do some internal recon."

"But why al-Jihad himself?" O'Reilly wondered

aloud, then shook his head. "Never mind. What else did you find?"

"A timetable of sorts." Romo brought up the message on-screen. "Even decrypted, it's couched in double-speak. You'll probably want to have the pros go over it, see if they're seeing what I am." He pointed out a couple of key phrases he thought referred to the planned jail-break, along with what he thought was a schedule. "Which means that if I'm right," he continued, "and if they're still on this same schedule, we're less than a day away from the jailbreak."

O'Reilly cursed under his breath. "You got any idea how it's going to go down?"

"No details," Romo said with ill-concealed regret. "There are a couple of references I can't place. Maybe your agents will be able to provide some insight."

"I'll get it right over to them." O'Reilly stuck his head out into the hallway and barked some orders. Moments later, the laptop was whisked away by two heavily armed, grim-faced men. O'Reilly himself, though, stayed behind in the office. "We're getting somewhere, at least."

The senior agent's body thrummed with barely re-strained eagerness, and some of the lines in his face had eased. That, more than anything, proved to Romo that O'Reilly was the right man for the job at hand. Although a few years older than the average field operative, the senior agent was clearly chafing at the Cell's recent lack of action, and the knowledge gaps that had ren-dered the task force unable to respond to the growing terror threat. That was why Romo had agreed to fake his own death and go undercover, he remembered now. Not just because it had been the right thing to do, but because he'd believed in his backup.

Hoping he wouldn't find out that his belief had been misplaced, Romo said, "Al-Jihad gave me forty-eight hours to return the flash drive to him. I don't know why he wants the thing back, or why he gave me so long to retrieve it, but if—and that's a big assumption, granted— he truly wants the thing back, we might be able to use it as bait."

O'Reilly regarded him steadily. "What did you have in mind?"

Romo lifted a shoulder. "We're running out of time to figure out what else is on the drive that he's so anxious to recover—frankly I don't see it, period, which makes me think the countdown was intended to get me focused on the wrong things."

"Misdirection." O'Reilly nodded. "It's consistent with al-Jihad's overall actions over the past eighteen months. Hell, the FBI didn't catch the significance of the hidden flash drive until it was almost too late. They were so busy trying to protect Mawadi's ex-wife, they let him get away with the drive."

Romo remembered that part of the investigation, and knew there had also been some infighting within the federal arm of the task force, and an affair between Mariah and her FBI protector, Grayson, which had further complicated things. But again, that had been the nature of al-Jihad's plans all along: sleight of hand and, as O'Reilly had said, misdirection.

"So what if we do some misdirection of our own?" Romo suggested.

O'Reilly's eyes narrowed with interest. "What do you have in mind?"

"I'm not sure yet." Romo thought for a moment, frowning. "Al-Jihad's men tried to kill me, to keep me from escaping from them in the woods. I get that. What I don't get is why they didn't move in on me while I was at Sara's, but instead went after Fax and McDermott before I could make contact in person. Then, instead of chasing me down, they herded me to the old apartment, where they'd planted a message that gave me enough clues to break the amnesia." He glossed over Sara's involvement in that aspect, hoping to keep her out of trouble. "Which suggests they knew about the amnesia somehow and wanted me to get my memory back. But why? The first thing I did was bring you guys the flash drive." He stalled, sucking in a breath. "Which might mean…"

"He wanted us to learn about the tunnels, but feel clever about it," O'Reilly said, then cursed viciously under his breath. "So we have to go on the assumption that either it's another misdirection, or it's a hell of an ambush."

"Or both," Romo muttered.

Before O'Reilly could say anything else, the office door swung open to reveal one of the heavily armed men, looking even grimmer than before. His eyes flicked to Romo and away.

"What's wrong?" Romo asked, surging up from the desk chair as every warning bell he possessed started clamoring all at once. "What happened?"

The agent looked at O'Reilly, who said, "I'll be right

there." The younger agent nodded and hurried from the room without looking at Romo, making him wonder whether the emergency had something to do with him, or whether he simply wasn't in the circle of trust.

"Come on," O'Reilly ordered, gesturing for Romo to join him and the other agent as they headed for what proved to be a conference room with a podium at one end and a long table. There were already a number of other Cell members seated at the table, a disparate half-dozen men who were very different in their outward appearances, ranging from a slick business type to a big guy who borderlined on thug territory. Romo was surprised to see Fairfax at the far end, looking paler than his usual tough-guy routine, and sporting a line of stitches along his scalp, but seeming otherwise okay. Romo sketched a small wave, got an even smaller, cool-eyed nod in return and figured he'd have to be satisfied with that.

If Sara's friends had been inclined to be angry with him for dumping her, he could only imagine how they felt about him now. But at the same time, he wasn't planning on letting that stop him from going after what he wanted. Not this time. He wanted all this to be over so he could go to her, sit her down and clear the air. Yes, he needed her to be flexible, but he needed to give her a better reason to take that chance. Simply demanding it wasn't enough, he'd realized.

He only hoped he hadn't realized it too late.

After O'Reilly closed and locked the door, and turned on some sort of scrambler apparatus that sat in the center of the long table, the meeting began. There were no introductions made, no real explanations before the slick-looking guy got up at the front of the room, pushed a couple of buttons and brought up a schematic that made Romo freeze in place. He was admittedly no expert, but the picture looked an awful lot like a large air-to-ground missile.

Slick said, "Based on our heuristic analysis of the transmissions Detective Sampson was able to decrypt, we believe the terrorists have acquired an incendiary bomb, and have placed it in the tunnel system very near the prison."

O'Reilly cursed bitterly. "Why are we just now hearing about this?" Then he shook his head. "Never mind. The how and why isn't important right now, not on this tight a timeline. Tell me what we know, and what we're going to do about it."

Over the next fifteen minutes, Slick—who Romo learned was actually named Wilson—went over the sparse details the Cell had managed to amass, which summed up to a very grim picture. The device, if it was what they thought it was, would crater the hell out of the tunnel system and the prison, killing everyone within either location. Al-Jihad had apparently named his successor within his terror organization, and a transmission intercepted only minutes earlier suggested that, in the event that the jailbreak failed, al-Jihad intended to martyr himself while making the explosion look as if it had been part of an FBI attack on the tunnel system and the prison itself, thereby inflaming the passions of terror leaders worldwide, and achieving his desired end of uniting America's enemies against her.

The concept was all the more chilling because none of the gathered agents was willing to say it wouldn't work.

Soon, the meeting moved into a response planning phase, and it became clear why O'Reilly had wanted Romo sitting in. He asked about numbers and thought processes, and about the men Romo had met personally during his months stuck in the crummy little apartment. If the senior agent had asked him going in whether he'd be able to help or not, Romo would've said no. But it turned out that he knew more than he thought, and the small details the Cell agents managed to pull from him helped shape the beginnings of a planned attack on the tunnel system. Other groups—including the FBI and BCCPD—would be brought in when the time came, of course, but for the moment, O'Reilly made it very clear that the plans stayed within that one room, period.

At the hour mark, once things had gone well beyond his areas of expertise, Romo held up a hand. When O'Reilly acknowledged him, he said, "No offense, but I don't think you guys need me here for this. I'd like to take another crack at the files on the flash drive, see if I couldn't find something we're all missing, some reason why al-Jihad would want to ensure that he got the copies back before launching the attack."

"Of course. The laptop is back in my office." O'Reilly tossed the key card to his office and waved him from the room, calling an absent thanks as the Cell members returned to their strategizing.

Romo found his way back to O'Reilly's office, used the key card to let himself in and sat back down at the computer. But he'd be damned if he could see what he was missing. There had to be some reason al-Jihad let him live as long as he had.

Staring intently at the files he'd pulled from the terrorist leader's computer, he muttered, "What if—"

A digital burble sounded, interrupting his half-formed thought. It took him a moment to remember the disposable phone he and Sara had been using. He pressed the button to answer, remembering that they'd only used it to call Sara's friends, and O'Reilly himself. The phone lacked caller ID, but since O'Reilly was just down the hall, Romo had to assume it was Fax's fiancée, whom Sara had called on the phone the day before. "Hello?" he said into the small unit. "Chelsea?"

There was a long pause before a soft voice said, "Romo, I'm in trouble. I need you to listen carefully and not freak out. Okay?"

It was Sara. And her tone left no doubt that there was something very badly wrong.

Adrenaline surged through Romo, jolting him to fight mode in an instant. There would be no "flight" this time. He only had "fight" left in him when it came to her. But, mindful of what she'd said, he marshaled his immediate response, "I'm listening. Go ahead."

His heart drummed against his ribs in the seemingly endless silence that followed his words. Then, finally, she said, "The men who were supposed to be taking me to the safe house were loyal to Jane Doe. Do you understand?"

He closed his eyes on a spear of panic so acute it was like pain. "I understand." She'd been taken. She'd trusted his word that she'd be safe, and she'd been kidnapped instead. Damn them.

"You need to come to the tunnel entrance. If you're not here in an hour, I'm dead."

The bald pronouncement speared through him, though of course that was the terrorists' modus operandi. "I'll be there," he promised, knowing damn well the location was closer to two hours away driving the legal limit. "What do they want me to bring?" he asked, still thinking he'd misconstrued al-Jihad's reference to wanting information from him.

"Nothing. Just yourself." Her voice was fading and strengthening, wavering, though he didn't know whether it was because she was injured or because someone was holding the phone to her mouth at an inconsistent distance. "Don't tell anyone where you're going or why. No messages, no clues. Just get up and walk out now. You're being watched."

A chill raced through him alongside confusion, but he didn't dare ask for clarification. Her voice and his own gut instinct told him they didn't have much time left on the call. "I'll be there, sweetheart."

He practically choked on the last word. Maybe it was a bad move calling her that, as it would clue any listeners in to their relationship. But he needed her to hear it, needed her to believe in him, in them. And besides, al-Jihad had been a step or two ahead of law enforcement all along. He had to know she was important to Romo.

Forget "important," he thought angrily, realizing he was once again minimizing his feelings for the sake of his own emotional safety. The terrorists already knew he'd do anything to protect her. She was the one who needed to hear it from him. "I love you, Sara," he said finally, his voice catching on the words. "Do you hear me? I. Love. You."

There was no answer. The phone had gone dead.

Chapter Eleven

Silent tears tracked down Sara's cheeks as Jane snapped the phone shut and tucked it into the pocket of her suit, which was navy, fitted and totally at odds with the tan fatigues worn by the three heavily armed men who had escorted them to the tunnel mouth for the phone call.

The day was sunny and cool, the sky a deep, cloudless blue. Sara stared up as a hawk passed overhead, and panic lumped in her throat at the sudden certainty that once she went back down into the tunnels, she wouldn't ever be coming back out.

"Come on." Jane headed back down into the tunnel, trusting the armed guards to bring Sara and not caring whether she came willingly or had to be dragged kicking and screaming. The former covert operative had already made it very clear to Sara that she didn't care what it took as long as the job got done. In this case, the job consisted of getting Romo out to the tunnels, though Sara wasn't clear on why that was so necessary. From what she'd seen inside the tunnel system in the hour or so since she'd awakened from her drugged stupor, the terrorists were horrifyingly well organized, well funded and well stocked for the planned attack on the ARX Supermax. What did they need Romo for?

When the guards closed in on Sara, she raised her hands in surrender. "I'm going." She'd tried resisting when they'd come to bring her to the surface for the phone call, and one of the men, without changing his expression an iota, had slammed his rifle butt into her stomach. While she'd been doubled over, retching, he'd grabbed her arm and force-marched her along the tunnel. Having no desire to waste her strength repeating that futile effort at rebellion, Sara followed Jane along the corridor-like tunnel that had been bored into the earth itself. The tunnel was lit by fluorescent lights bolted to the rock ceiling at regular intervals, and conduits and wires ran along one side, bundled together and branching off into each intersecting tunnel they passed.

Sara was following orders, but she was also waiting for her chance to run. She might be nothing more than a doctor who—as Romo had unkindly but accurately pointed out—hadn't even had the guts to treat living patients, but she damn well wasn't going to sit by and let the terrorists destroy her home. Not if there was anything she could do to prevent it.

Her mother had eventually come to grips with her sham of a marriage and the wounds it was inflicting on Sara. She'd gotten a divorce, and met and married a sturdy, good-hearted man who would give her the world if he could. Sara had been grateful for her stepfather, and had maintained a relationship of sorts with her father, who hadn't remarried, but instead floated from affair to affair. Her parents had found their places eventually.

Maybe she had, too.

The problem was, she didn't have a clue what to do, or how. She needed help. She needed Romo, she thought, on a mix of fear and wistful hope that he could somehow manage to slip a rescue past Jane and the agent who was supposedly still acting within the antiterror group Jane had once led, feeding her information on Romo's progress and movements. But there was little hope of that, Sara knew. And if he tried some sort of heroics, Jane had said, Sara was dead. The ex-agent turned traitor was an elegant woman in her early forties, made up and well put together. But she was icy cold, and all but radiated purposeful evil. Sara didn't doubt her word for one second. If it came down to it, Jane would kill her without hesitation.

The knowledge was a hard knot in Sara's stomach, but she forced herself to hold it together, trying to keep track of the tunnel's turns they made on the way down from the surface. Just in case.

Men—and a few women, but only a few—moved through the tunnels with quick, purposeful strides. Some wore tan fatigues, others street clothes. Most were armed. None met Sara's eyes.

The realization brought a renewed chill.

Focus, she told herself. *Look for things you can use, things that might be important.* She had to keep thinking about her escape, keep planning for it, because if she didn't, she thought she would break down.

She counted hallways, saw hollowed-out chambers containing piles of equipment, one filled with a strange piece of machinery that looked like something out of a science fiction movie. Before she could fully register the apparatus, Jane continued onward, but waved for the guards to peel off. They prodded Sara into the same chamber she'd awakened in. The vaguely rectangular room seemed to have been part of an offshoot tunnel at some point, but now was capped off at either end with huge steel plating that extended from floor to ceiling and was set into grooves on either side. There was a door in one of the slabs; after pushing her through, the guards stepped out and locked her in, leaving her alone.

She stumbled to the far side of the room, where there was a single folding chair and a half-full bottle of water that had been that way when she'd awakened. At the time, she'd been disgusted by the thought of drinking a stranger's backwash. Now she downed the liquid gratefully, replenishing the hydration lost to the drugs, and the weakness of tears.

Those tears were done with now, she told herself. She needed to pull it together and figure out her best course of action. She hated that Jane was using her to bring Romo to the tunnels, where God only knew what would happen to him. But she had an hour, maybe less, before he arrived. What if she could get free before then, meet him at the entrance with information on the tunnels, manpower and equipment?

It might be an unlikely scenario, but it was one that gave her a buzz of hope. She needed to believe that she would see him again, that they would have a chance to talk about what had happened back at the hotel. Not just the lovemaking—though she had a few things to say to him on that score—but what he'd said about her needing to want him enough to find a way to forgive him. Maybe that wasn't exactly what he'd said, but that was what she'd taken away from the fight, and that was what she'd thought about after she'd regained consciousness, while she'd huddled in the chill, sparsely furnished room accompanied only by her thoughts.

She'd thought about Romo. And she'd realized he'd been right. Not about all of it, certainly. But he'd been right about enough of it that she'd been forced to admit he hadn't single-handedly destroyed their relationship. She'd played a part in its deconstruction, too. And in the end, if fidelity had been a test for him, then commitment had been a challenge for her. She'd held part of herself away from him, as though she'd been waiting all along for him to make the mistake he eventually had. Yes, he'd deliberately chosen to do something he knew she wouldn't be able to forgive…but she'd let him know in so many little ways that she was waiting for it to happen. In the end, while that didn't make his actions right, it did make her fears something of a self-fulfilling prophecy.

Neither of them had been blameless, by a long shot. And in reality, maybe that was the take-home of their former relationship. Maybe they hadn't been ready for what they'd found together. She might've thought she was at the time, but she hadn't been, not really.

She was now, though. In losing him she'd found a part of herself that had been missing before—the part that now told her she had to fight for him, no matter what it took. Which also meant fighting for Bear Claw, because there was no way the two of them could move forward unless Jane Doe, al-Jihad and the others were brought to justice, once and for all.

"Which sounds great in theory, but is going to be hard as hell to pull off in practice," she said aloud. Nonetheless, she had to do something.

Gritting her teeth, she lunged to her feet, grabbed the folding chair and slammed it into the wall. She screamed as she swung, not caring who heard her, not caring what they thought. The impact reverberated up her arm and stung her hands as the chair crumpled and dented. She ignored the discomfort and swung again. And again.

On the fourth swing, one leg started to tear free, leaving a jaggedly pointed end. On the sixth smashing blow it came free, and she had herself a pry bar. And a weapon.

Heart pounding, she set to work, hoping to hell that she and Romo wouldn't miss each other again. Their timing had been off before. She didn't intend to let it be off again, because this time, getting it wrong could get both of them—and many innocents—very dead.

A few months ago, that knowledge would've sent her into hiding. Now it just made her work faster.

ROMO SLIPPED FROM THE BUILDING where the Cell was headquartered, took a cab to the lot where he'd left his truck days earlier and considered himself lucky to find the vehicle still waiting for him, keys hidden where he'd left them. Inwardly, he was on the brink of panic. Outwardly, he forced himself calm, made himself do what needed to be done. He paid the cabdriver, got in the truck and navigated out of the city, moving fast but keeping it close enough to legal that he didn't find himself pulled over.

Sweat prickled across his shoulder blades, itching along the stitches. His mind raced as he tried to figure out al-Jihad's plan. The terrorists didn't care about the flash drive anymore, that much was plain. But why did they want him? Was there yet more vital information locked behind an amnesiac block? He didn't think so—he felt as though he'd gotten it all back, remembering what he'd needed and wanted to remember. Was it a case of simple revenge? Al-Jihad might be seeking to maintain face at having been taken in by an undercover operative who not only wasn't trained for undercover work, he wasn't even a true operative, merely an internal affairs detective who'd gotten an offer he'd told himself he couldn't refuse.

That scenario played, he supposed. But it didn't offer much hope for his or Sara's safety.

Romo cursed under his breath as he cleared the city limits and hit the gas, spiking the odometer well past eighty miles per hour, edging toward ninety as he headed hell-bent for the tunnel entrance. *What do they want?* he kept asking himself. More, how was he going to get Sara to safety without hinting to the terrorists that the Cell and other agencies were strategizing an attack?

He didn't know, and the lack of a plan had him beyond worried. He'd done his best to alert O'Reilly that there was a serious problem, leaving the senior agent's office in disarray on his way out. He hadn't dared leave a note, because he had to believe that there were still more conspirators within the Cell. Which meant there really wasn't anyone he *could* trust at this point, didn't it?

Sara trusted Fax, he remembered. O'Reilly also trusted him. And, if he was really honest with himself, Romo realized that on some level he trusted the big, brooding agent, too. Even injured, he was more backup than Romo'd had in many months.

As he blasted along the highway, Romo waged an inner war. The instructions Sara had relayed, coming from Jane Doe and the terrorists, had been explicit— tell no one. But he couldn't do this alone. He needed help, not just to get Sara to safety, but to avert al-Jihad's terrible plan.

Cursing bitterly, Romo yanked out his phone, re-called the last number dialed off the disposable phone and hit Send. When a woman's voice answered, he said, "I need Fax's cell number, right now."

"Who is this?" Chelsea responded, immediately suspicious.

He hesitated the briefest instant before he said, clearly and calmly, "This is Romo. My death was faked. I've been undercover the whole time with al-Jihad's people, except for the past week, when I've been living with Sara, trying to keep us both alive. I messed up, though, big-time. Jane Doe has Sara in a set of mining tunnels north of the prison. I'm meeting them there, I need help and I don't know who else I can trust." He paused, and when there was no response, he tossed his damned pride out the window and said, "I know you don't have any reason to trust or believe me at this point, not after the funeral, and after what happened between me and Sara. But please, for her sake, help me. Give me Fax's damn number."

This time there was barely a pause before she said, "I'll do better than that. Tell me exactly where this tunnel is."

It was a test, he knew. A challenge. His trust for hers. Before, he would've hung up. Now he took a deep breath, and told her, finishing with, "Tell Fax there's someone inside the Cell funneling reports to Jane Doe. So he's got to be absolutely sure of anyone he talks to."

"Understood," Chelsea said briskly, all business now. "Promise me that you'll wait for us?"

"I—" He broke off, went with the truth. "I'd promise you, but it'd be a lie. I'm going to get there and see what the situation looks like. If I need to go in to keep Sara alive, that's what I'm going to do, and I'll be keeping my fingers crossed that you guys get there in time to haul us out if things go bad."

He reached the highway exit leading into the back-country. Letting up on the gas only slightly, he sent the truck roaring in the direction he needed to go. The cheap cell started to hiss and spit as Chelsea said, "You always did go your own way, Detective."

"You'll help?"

"Of course. See you there." Chelsea cut the call, leaving Romo hoping he hadn't just made the most costly mistake of his—and Sara's—life. But if he'd demanded that she learn to be more flexible, he had to give the same in return, which meant asking for help when he needed it. Like now. He'd told her to have faith in him, but it wasn't fair to ask for something he wasn't willing to give.

Working off the map that had been on the flash drive, the details of which were seared into his brain thanks to his near-perfect recall of math, computer and engineering stuff, Romo turned onto a narrow dirt track leading into the scrubby woodlands that made up the outlying tracts of the Bear Claw Creek State Forest. The undeveloped land was state-owned but not part of the park itself, which meant it wasn't ranger-patrolled and didn't get much attention. Although the land around the prison was secured for several miles in each direction, the tunnel system began outside that range, which was undoubtedly why al-Jihad's plan had gone undetected for so long. That, along with some help from the new prison warden, Weberly.

It was simultaneously an intricate plan and a damnably simple one, Romo thought, still unable to figure out why the terrorists wanted him there. Vengeance was certainly a possibility, but it seemed a risky conceit at this point in al-Jihad's plan. Regardless, Romo kept the gas pinned to the floor, sending the truck hurtling up the dirt road because there wasn't another option as far as he was concerned. He'd left Sara twice before, once when he'd betrayed her with another woman, and again when he'd faked his own death. He wouldn't do it a third time. He was done running away.

By the time he was within sight of the tunnel mouth,

he was a good twenty minutes over the time he'd been given. Short of hijacking a helicopter, there hadn't been any way to get there sooner, though. He hoped to hell the terrorists recognized that, and had given him the deadline to ensure that he left the Cell building in a hurry.

The tunnel mouth was empty, though. There didn't seem to be anyone waiting for him. Had they decided he wasn't coming? Had they—

"No," he said aloud. "Don't even go there." Palming the cheap phone, he tried to return Sara's call, but couldn't get a signal. No doubt the phone she'd called out on had been a slicker model with a stronger signal— a satellite phone or the like.

Muttering a curse, he jammed the disposable phone in his pocket and parked the truck. After hiding the key, he strode toward the tunnel, hoping to hell nothing had gone badly wrong in the nearly hour and a half it'd taken him to reach the meeting point.

"Hello?" he called when he reached the tunnel, which proved to be a rocky conduit liberally braced with timeworn timbers that had been reinforced with new-looking metal, presumably when al-Jihad took over the tunnel system. When there was no answer but the echo of Romo's own voice, he moved into the tunnel. "Sara?" he called softly. "I'm here, sweetheart."

A rustle of motion from behind him had him spinning and raising his fists in defense. He found himself staring down the barrel of an autopistol held by a stone-faced man in tan fatigues.

He nearly leaped at the guy, as his blood drummed with the need to get to Sara, to make sure she was okay.

But he controlled the impulse and forced himself to hold out his hands, showing that he was unarmed. "I'm just trying to get to my meeting, understand? I'm not looking to make trouble. I just want my woman back." It was partly a lie, partly the truth. He most definitely did intend to make trouble, but he intended to get Sara to safety before he did. "Take me to Jane Doe. Please."

A hard blow caught Romo from behind, driving him to his knees. He bellowed in pain, tried to spin and meet the new attack, but lost his equilibrium and fell instead. The next few seconds were a blur of kicks and punches, with Romo taking far more of them than he managed to dish out. He cursed and scrabbled, fighting dirty, but the two guards subdued him, binding his hands behind him and securing the knot to a tight nylon rope that ran around his throat, biting into his windpipe. It was a simple system, but all too effective. If he didn't keep his bound hands high up between his shoulder blades, the rope dug in and he started choking. Add in the pain from his healing wound, and he was unable to do much more than curse as the guards searched him roughly, pocketed his phone, then dragged him into the tunnel system. As the artificial light of the fluorescent tube–lit tunnel closed in around him and the view of blue skies and freedom disappeared, Romo found himself hoping to hell that Chelsea was as good as her word, because he had a feeling he was going to need backup badly, and soon.

After a forced march of five minutes, maybe longer, during which he tried to keep track of his location relative to the schematic in his head, the guards yanked him to a halt just outside a steel-paneled doorway. One held a gun on him while the other unlatched the door and swung it open.

A blur erupted from the other side of the doorway, screaming and swinging something in a lethal arc. There was a sick thud and the guard nearest the door went down.

Part of Romo froze in shock and fear when he realized the blur was Sara, that she'd just ambushed one of al-Jihad's guards with what looked like a leg off a damned folding chair. Fortunately, though, the instincts that had brought him through months of treacherous undercover work were still close to the surface, and had him head-butting the second guard even as the first one went down. He caught his guard in the split second of shocked distraction when Sara attacked. The guy's gun went flying. A second head butt sent him folding to the ground, though Romo nearly choked himself to death in the process.

He folded, gagging.

"Romo!" Sara was at his side in a second, quickly untying his bonds.

"Thanks," he said, his voice rough with a whole lot of emotions that had no place just then, as he and Sara grabbed the guards and dragged them into the cell where she'd been held. "Nice job."

"Thanks," she said, breathless. "Are they—"

"They'll live." At least until al-Jihad or Jane Doe learned of their mistake. Then all bets were off. He didn't say that, though. Instead he said, "Help me get their uniforms off." She frowned but didn't argue, and they quickly pulled the tan fatigue shirts on over their own.

"Pants, too?" she asked.

He shook his head. "Shirts only, in case we need to lose them quickly." As in, he didn't want to be mistaken for the wrong side if—no, when—backup arrived, whether it was Fax and the others, or the entire Cell-backed response, traitors and all.

Once they had their disguises in place, Romo guided Sara back out into the hallway and shut and locked the door on the unconscious guards. Then he turned to her and gave himself a second to stare, memorizing the sight of her and beginning to believe he'd made it this far, at the very least. "You're okay?"

"Scared and furious, but generally unharmed." Her words were flip, but she was staring at him with an intensity equal to his own. "You came alone?"

He was tempted to tell her that backup was theoretically on the way, but he didn't dare tip his hand if there was surveillance. And besides, that wasn't what he wanted to tell her in the scant seconds before they had to be on the move. So he said simply, "I came for you."

"Oh," she said on a quick inhale. A wash of color touched her pale face, and she lifted the broken chair leg, which was wickedly pointed at one end. "I was coming out to help you."

"I think that makes us even." Knowing it wasn't the time or place for deeper revelations, he dropped a quick kiss on her lips, scooped up the men's guns and handed her one. "Come on. Let's get out of here."

They moved through the tunnels without incident, with Romo leading the way. They were less than half-way out when sirens erupted and all hell broke loose.

The tramp of booted feet rang out nearby, along with men's shouts of alarm, with a cool, commanding female voice rapping out orders over the din, then snapping, "I don't care. *Find them!"*

Sara grabbed Romo, dragging at him. "That's Jane! She must've realized we escaped."

He nodded, heart and mind racing. Sara's safety was his priority, but what if their escape had just created a larger problem? What if al-Jihad decided the risk was too great, and triggered the bomb outright? If that happened, there wouldn't be any place safe within a dozen miles of the tunnels.

"We're going to have to run for it," he said, hefting the autopistol and hoping to hell he didn't have to kill anyone on the way out. He didn't want her to see that side of him, had hoped to never have to use it again.

She tightened her fingers on his. "I'm right behind you."

He moved out, and didn't look back.

They hurried along a long hallway that paralleled the one the guards had brought him down. Romo heard the shouts and footsteps of search parties, and the rumble of what sounded a great deal like heavy equipment, which made him wonder if the terrorists still had digging to do, or if they had moved up the prison break for some reason. Thinking of O'Reilly's timetable, he cursed under his breath. If Fax didn't come through—

No, he couldn't worry about that now. He had to concentrate on getting him and Sara the hell out of the tunnels.

When they reached a crossway, Romo hesitated, then turned away from the loudest noises of search and pursuit, even knowing it tacked them away from the surface. His mind raced as he went over the map in his head, trying to figure out where they were, where they could go. If they were where he thought, then there should be another cross tunnel—there! Moving fast, he tugged Sara toward what ought to be a shortcut to the surface.

He rounded the corner, leading with the autopistol. Seeing nothing in the dim tunnel ahead, he moved into the smaller shaft, ducking to clear the single string of bare bulbs that lit the space. "Come on," he whispered almost soundlessly. "This should lead out."

The sounds of pursuit faded. Hope started to stir in his chest, hastening his steps. He kept his weapon up, though, stayed alert for problems as they sped along the tunnel.

Moving too fast, he passed a cross-tunnel that shouldn't have been there, at least according to the map. Motion blurred in his peripheral vision and his instincts shrilled a warning, but it was already too late. A shadowy figure lunged out of the tunnel as he spun. The tan-clad guard slammed into him, grabbed his wrist and bashed his gun hand against the rock wall of the tunnel, sending the weapon skittering away.

Growling near-feral denial that their escape had been foiled so close to success, keeping his voice low so they wouldn't attract attention from the other searchers, Romo grappled with the guard and hissed, "Go, Sara. Run!"

But he heard her shriek, heard another struggle nearby and realized she'd been grabbed, too. Knowing there was nothing to be gained from silence now, Romo howled and fought his attacker, shouting rage and fury at the top of his lungs, in the hopes that Fax and the others would hear.

But there was no response, no backup. The guard slammed a stiff-armed punch into Romo's temple, leaving him dazed. His head spun and the world lurched as the guards dragged him to his feet and he was once again force-marched back into the warren of tunnels, this time with Sara right behind him. He cursed bitterly in his soul, hoping to hell he could figure a way out of this mess, fearing he might not be able to.

That fear intensified to near certainty when the guards shoved him through a doorway into a larger, well-lit room that held two men—al-Jihad and Lee Mawadi—one woman—Jane Doe—and one seriously nasty-looking piece of machinery...the incendiary bomb.

Chapter Twelve

Sara's head spun and her stomach pitched at the sight confronting her and Romo. If she'd been free to move, she would've grabbed his arm and clung, not out of terror, though she was thoroughly terrified, but to prevent him from breaking away from the man who held him, and flinging himself at the assembled group in some sort of mad suicide rush. He didn't, though. He stood fast and glared at the man in the center of the room.

Al-Jihad was square-shouldered and dark-eyed, and carried an aura of command like a second skin. Jane Doe stood on one side of the terrorist mastermind. On his other side was a blond, good-looking man who wore tan fatigues along with an air of deadly menace. Sara was pretty sure he was the last of the escapees, terrorist Lee Mawadi, whom Fax had described as being somewhat lacking in initiative, but not in killer instincts. More, since Mawadi's ex-wife, Mariah Shore, had been put well out of his reach under the watchful eyes of her new lover, FBI task force agent Michael Grayson, Mawadi had been increasingly associated with the most deadly of the smaller incidents in and around Bear Claw. Sara had heard Fax say that Mawadi was on a downward spiral. She could easily believe that, based on the mad glee in the man's eyes and his possessive stance near the huge missile-like contraption that took up half the room and could only be, even to her disbelieving, untrained eyes, a bomb.

Sara clamped her lips against a whimper that came from both fear and discomfort as the man holding her twisted her arm a little higher behind her back.

Not looking at her, Romo faced al-Jihad, his jaw set. "I came like you told me to. Let the woman go."

It was Jane who answered coolly, "That wasn't the deal."

Romo flicked a glance at her. "Then what *was* the deal?"

"O'Reilly is planning an attack," she said. "I want the details, and I want them now."

"You've got someone inside the Cell already. Why not ask them?"

"Your girlfriend's guards were the last two upper-level operatives loyal to me, and I needed them to bring me my leverage." Jane nodded in Sara's direction. "Even at their level, O'Reilly wasn't bringing them in on the really hot stuff—he kept that to him, Fairfax and a few others. My one remaining asset inside is way out of the loop—she told me there were meetings, maybe a plan, but couldn't get anything more. That's why you're here. We needed someone inside the circle of trust."

"You…" Romo trailed off, expression firming. "Son of a—this was what you were planning all along, wasn't it?"

Al-Jihad said, "This was one of the eventualities, yes. We projected that once you escaped, you would eventually return to O'Reilly, and that he would bring you into his confidence once we added the pressure of the flash drive. We didn't care about the maps. We wanted you back inside the Cell Block, and that was the simplest way to get you there." His eyes flicked to Sara. "And we knew you were vulnerable. Since Fairfax put his woman out of our reach, you were the next best option."

"Plans within plans," Romo muttered. "We knew that much, but didn't see where they were headed."

"The same place they've been going all along," Mawadi said with a sneer on his face and in his voice. "Toward victory. In less than an hour, we will have breached the ARX. With the help of our men on the inside, we're going to unleash hell on your earth." His lips turned up in a smile of pure joy that looked so very wrong on a man who had grown up in a middle-class family and gone to an Ivy League school, where he'd found a series of anti-American groups that had provided an outlet for his anger and sociopathic tendencies.

Sara shuddered involuntarily. She'd been afraid before, when Jane had forced her to make the phone call. Now, though, she knew they were at the end of things, and she was terrified. The immediate future of Bear Claw and many of the people she loved rested on what she and Romo did in the next few minutes.

"Don't tell them anything," she blurted. "Don't."

After a glance back at the man who held him with an autopistol stuck in his side, Romo turned to her. His eyes were cool and steady, though she saw a layer of anguish beneath. "I won't let them hurt you. I love you."

At times in the past, she would've given anything to hear those words, under any circumstance. Now, though, she found herself flaring. Anger spiked. "Don't you *dare!*" she blazed, taking a step toward him. The guard holding her must've been surprised—or amused—by her response, because he let her go, though kept his gun trained on her. Sara continued, her volume increasing. "Don't even think you can make this be about you and me. I'm not asking you to tell them anything. Hell, I forbid it. You say you love me? Well, that's too little too late, given that you've spent the past couple of years proving otherwise. So prove it now. Don't tell them a damn thing."

"Sara, listen—"

"Stop it!" Heart thudding sickly in her chest, she rounded on him, moving in and getting in his face, keeping the attention centered on their fight, knowing they didn't have much more time before the guards broke it up. Almost screaming now, hoping the flare in his eyes meant that he'd caught on, she railed, "And don't you dare say you love me now."

He took a step back, face blanking as he jostled against his guard. "Look, sweetheart, I didn't mean— *get down!*" Breaking off, he spun on his guard and went for the autopistol.

Sara flung herself flat and scrambled behind the big machine as shouts rang out and men grappled. Only then did it occur to her that she'd taken shelter behind a really big bomb. She didn't know what would trigger it, hoped it wasn't twitchy.

"Don't shoot!" Jane snapped, apparently thinking the same thing. "Not in here."

The guards piled on Romo, punching and kicking, while Jane and Lee Mawadi broke for the door. Al-Jihad, though, headed straight for Sara. Or rather, straight for the bomb.

She saw the mad fury in his eyes, along with a calm fatality that scared her far more than almost anything else she'd seen or experienced in her life. Once before, when she'd been unable to avoid hearing her friends talking about the case, Fax had said, "There's nothing more dangerous than a true believer." She hadn't gotten it at the time. Now she understood.

Al-Jihad was not only willing to kill thousands of Americans on behalf of his cause. He was willing to die for it himself, and thought he was doing what was right and just.

His eyes met hers as he reached for a keypad inset into the side of the device. She saw in his expression, disconcertingly, a profound and gentle sadness. He tapped a couple of keys, and a subsonic whine began.

He was going to kill them all.

"No!" Sara lunged out from behind the machine and slammed into al-Jihad, sending him staggering a few steps back.

Taller and bigger than she by far, the terrorist leader bellowed and grabbed her, tossing her aside. She hit the wall hard and slid down it. Dazed, she heard gunshots out in the hallway, and a commotion.

Romo roared her name and fought his way toward her. Dragging her up, he gripped her tight for a moment, his skin hot against hers. Then he pushed her at someone else. "Take her. Get her out of here. Get *everyone* out of here!"

Her head cleared as someone grabbed her and started hustling her away. She saw the guards motionless on the ground, one bleeding, saw Lee Mawadi hissing and spitting, struggling as a tall, gray-eyed man in a suit and Kevlar cuffed him roughly, his face etched with hatred. Jane Doe, unconscious and handcuffed, was being hauled out over the shoulder of a big man in SWAT gear.

The cavalry had arrived, Sara realized, and they were in mop-up-and-retreat mode. Which meant they thought the bomb was going to go off.

Yet Romo was staying behind.

"No!" She struggled and fought, trying to get back to Romo as he lunged for al-Jihad, who had returned to the keypad.

Then she was being dragged through the door and out into the hallway and someone was shouting her name. It took a moment for that to penetrate, another for her to focus and recognize the man who held her.

"Fax!" She gripped his forearms, saw him wince. "What are you doing here?"

"Your boyfriend finally wised up and called in a favor." Fax looked to where the others were hustling Jane Doe and Mawadi out of the tunnel system under a six-man guard. Gunfire barked intermittently in the distance, and she heard shouts and screams. "We got here just ahead of O'Reilly, and made a few adjustments to his plan."

"The bomb!" Sara said in horror, as the door to the bomb room swung shut and locked. *"Romo!"*

"Go!" Fax shoved her after the others. "Get out of here. I'll help him."

She wavered, knowing she couldn't help, but needing to be there, wanting, crazily, to be with him if the worst happened. "I don't—"

"Trust me," Fax said stolidly. His eyes darkened. "If you can't do that, then trust him. If anything happens to you that could've been prevented, dead or alive he'll never forgive himself."

She looked at Fax. "I thought you didn't like him."

"I don't have to like him. You're the one he's in love with."

Romo had said the words only moments earlier, and she'd tucked them next to her heart. Now, hearing it again, even from an outside source, the words expanded into a burgeoning warmth that suffused her, flowing through her on a burst of belief. "Yes," she said, a smile touching her lips. "I am." She sucked in a deep breath, pulled herself together and nodded. "I'm going. You help him."

She took off, and she didn't look back. She had to trust Romo, trust Fax, to bring down the terror leader who had kept Bear Claw locked in a state of suspended panic for nearly a year.

As she fled the tunnels, she passed other operatives coming in. One made a grab for her, no doubt because she was wearing the tan uniform shirt, but a woman's voice called, "Don't, she's with us!" Then Chelsea was there, short and curvy as ever, but these days wearing Kevlar and a tense, businesslike expression. Sara's former assistant waded toward her, grabbed her and pulled her outside, into the light of day, where the sun still shone down from a perfect blue sky, despite the danger down below.

"Romo's still in there." Sara gripped her friend's arms. "Fax is with him! We have to—"

"We have to let them do their jobs," Chelsea said, but her eyes were full of fear and anguish.

A gray-haired man Sara guessed was O'Reilly stood just outside the tunnel mouth, shouting orders. Vehicles were headed away from the site, undoubtedly racing to get outside the blast radius. Sara and Chelsea, though, looked at each other and stayed put, Chelsea shaking her head in a firm negative when O'Reilly sent a glare in their direction.

They were waiting for the men they loved, Sara thought, realizing that the word really, truly applied to her for the first time. She loved Romo. She didn't want to live without him. Been there, done that. More importantly, she believed in him, and in Fax. She believed, maybe for the first time, in love.

Fax and Chelsea had met because of al-Jihad. Sara and Romo had been separated because of him. She couldn't—wouldn't—believe it would end because of the terrorist leader.

Please, she thought in a prayerful moment, tightening her fingers on Chelsea's as the minutes ticked down and the activity at the tunnel mouth stilled. Nearby, terse reports filtered to O'Reilly's radio, noting that the new warden and his henchmen had been taken into custody, and the digging party poised to break through into the prison confines had been stopped and subdued. Helicopters lifted off on the other side of the low mountain, bearing the agents and terrorists wounded in the skirmish.

Then there was a flurry of activity at the tunnel mouth. Sara's heart leaped at the sight of two bedraggled men, one wearing Kevlar, the other a tan uniform shirt, emerge from the tunnel, dragging the limp form of al-Jihad between them.

"Romo!" she cried, with Chelsea only seconds behind her, shouting Fax's name. The women broke and ran to their men as a cheer went up at the sight of al-Jihad, recaptured at long last.

Bodies jammed the tunnel entrance as O'Reilly's trusted agents took control of al-Jihad, escorting him to a nearby vehicle under heavy guard. Sara was dimly aware that two other vehicles held Jane Doe and Lee Mawadi, while knots of tan-clad men, with a sprinkling of women, were being held within rings of armed agents, each overseen by a key member of the task force.

Those were peripheral inputs, though, far secondary to Sara's focus on the tall, dark-haired man who had moved to the edge of the scrum, gladly relinquishing control of his prisoner. He wasn't at the edge of the crowd because he didn't belong, though. Not anymore. No, he'd worked his way free because he was anxiously scanning, looking for someone. Looking, Sara knew, for her.

She called his name, but her words were lost in the din. Chelsea dove into the crowd, headed for Fax, and Sara angled to the edge, toward Romo.

He saw her and went still, his eyes locked on her.

She hesitated fractionally, unable to read his expression, which was somehow simultaneously fierce and gentle, angry and elated. As he moved to close the distance between them, anxiety rose from deep within her—old fears, old insecurities. Not about his commitment to her—she was finally past that, finally believed that he wouldn't just stay faithful to her, he wouldn't just die for her, he'd live for her, too. But about her own ability to make a long-term relationship work.

Then he reached her and they finally stood opposite each other, close enough to touch, as the chaos of the official response ebbed and flowed around them, somehow yielding an island of calm in the middle of the craziness.

"It's over," he said. "Thank God it's finally over."

"I trust you're referring to al-Jihad's reign of terror in Bear Claw, and not us," she said, her stomach knotted on the utter certainty that it was now or never for them.

Heat flared in the depths of Romo's eyes and he moved closer, seemed to grow larger, until he blocked out everything else around them with his presence, and with the certainty in his expression. "We are most definitely not over," he said, then paused with a quirk of one eyebrow, as though daring her to argue.

She said quickly, "I didn't mean most of what I said down there, you know. I was picking a fight to draw their attention."

His lips twitched. "Yeah, I got that. But I also know there was a bit of truth to all of it." When she would've protested, he held up a hand. "The other day, I demanded that you get over yourself and learn to be flexible, but I never really gave you any assurance that it'd be worth the change." He paused, his eyes going smoky. "I cheated. It wasn't because of you, or her, or anything but me and being all messed up in my own head, but that doesn't excuse the fact that I cheated. If anything, it makes it worse, because on some level I think I must've done it deliberately, as you said, to force you to dump me. I'm not proud of it. I'd take it back if I could. But I can't, so the best I can do is own it. I did it, and I swear on my soul that I will never cheat, ever again."

Sara had thought she'd gotten past their tumultuous history, had thought she was over the waitress. But she found, when her throat closed and tears filmed her eyes, that she hadn't been completely past it. She'd needed his promise, and hadn't even known it. But by the same token, she had something she owed back to him. "You were right about me, though. I was so used to thinking of relationships as being either perfect or complete failures, I didn't fight hard enough to work things out when the going got tough between us." She paused, then went with the rest of the honesty. "I think…I think I wasn't ready for you, didn't know how to deal with what I felt for you. I wanted everything to be calm and easy, and that's not real life."

Something uncoiled in his expression, in his body. The immediate bustle had died down, the prisoners had been driven away. Sara was aware of Fax and Chelsea standing nearby, twined together, completing each other. For a moment, Sara was reminded of sitting in her office—had it really been less than a week ago?—trying not to resent Chelsea's happiness. Now, Sara knew she was on the verge of claiming that same sort of happiness, if she could be strong enough to reach for it, and to make it work even when the rough patches came.

The tough stuff wasn't over, either. Bear Claw and the BCCPD were going to be headed into some serious mopping up, as the task force rooted out the last of the conspirators and the city headed for a special election that would—God willing—put in place a mayor she could actually work with, and who would work with her. But that didn't mean she should wait around until all that settled down to take what she wanted, did it?

Love wasn't about everything being perfect, she was starting to realize. It was about caring enough to make the imperfect moments work.

Romo's expression eased; a faint, hopeful smile touched his lips. He held out a hand to her. "Can I come home now?"

And then, finally, it was easy for Sara to take his hand, to smile up at him and say, "God, yes. I've missed you."

He drew her close, touched his lips to hers. "I love you."

Before, she'd yearned for the words. Now they were nothing more than a part of the whole. Still, though, they brought a warm, soft glow to her heart as she leaned into the kiss, and whispered, "I love you, too."

They kissed again, long and soft, and full of promises for tomorrow and the day after, on into the future. They didn't break apart until an officious throat clearing sounded, demanding attention.

It was Fax, grinning sardonically. "You two willing

to take it somewhere else?" He gestured to the growing crowd that now eddied around them, as a second wave of responders arrived and moved in on the crime scene.

Sara flushed, but smiled at her friends, then up at Romo. "Do you need to do anything more with O'Reilly?"

He shrugged. "I'm sure he'll track me down if and when he needs me. I have a feeling he's done with me for the time being, though."

The four friends turned away from the tunnels and the ARX Supermax, linked arm in arm as they headed back to Bear Claw. They, and the city itself, would start a new chapter now that the terror threat was ended.

Who knew what the future would hold? Sara thought, a bubble of exhilaration rising in her chest. Whatever the outcome, she knew, she and Romo would face it. Together.

* * * * *

*Celebrate 60 years of pure reading pleasure
with Harlequin®!*

To commemorate the event, Silhouette Special Edition invites you to Ashley O'Ballivan's bed-and-breakfast in the small town of Stone Creek. The beautiful innkeeper will have her hands full caring for her old flame Jack McCall. He's on the run and recovering from a mysterious illness, but that won't stop him from trying to win Ashley back.

*Enjoy an exclusive glimpse of Linda Lael Miller's
AT HOME IN STONE CREEK
Available in November 2009
from Silhouette Special Edition®.*

The helicopter swung abruptly sideways in a dizzying arch, setting Jack McCall's fever-ravaged brain spinning.

His friend's voice sounded tinny, coming through the earphones. "You belong in a hospital," he said. "Not some backwater bed-and-breakfast."

All Jack really knew about the virus raging through his system was that it wasn't contagious, and there was no known treatment for it besides a lot of rest and quiet. "I don't like hospitals," he responded, hoping he sounded like his normal self. "They're full of sick people."

Vince Griffin chuckled but it was a dry sound, rough at the edges. "What's in Stone Creek, Arizona?" he asked. "Besides a whole lot of nothin'?"

Ashley O'Ballivan was in Stone Creek, and she was a whole lot of somethin', but Jack had neither the strength nor the inclination to explain. After the way he'd ducked out six months before, he didn't expect a welcome, knew he didn't deserve one. But Ashley, being Ashley, would take him in whatever her misgivings.

He had to get to Ashley; he'd be all right.

He closed his eyes, letting the fever swallow him.

There was no telling how much time had passed when he became aware of the chopper blades slowing overhead. Dimly, he saw the private ambulance waiting on the airfield outside of Stone Creek; it seemed that twilight had descended.

Jack sighed with relief. His clothes felt clammy against his flesh. His teeth began to chatter as two figures unloaded a gurney from the back of the ambulance and waited for the blades to stop.

"Great," Vince remarked, unsnapping his seat belt. "Those two look like volunteers, not real EMTs."

The chopper bounced sickeningly on its runners, and Vince, with a shake of his head, pushed open his door and jumped to the ground, head down.

Jack waited, wondering if he'd be able to stand on his own. After fumbling unsuccessfully with the buckle on his seat belt, he decided not.

When it was safe the EMTs approached, following Vince, who opened Jack's door.

His old friend Tanner Quinn stepped around Vince, his grin not quite reaching his eyes.

"You look like hell warmed over," he told Jack cheerfully.

"Since when are you an EMT?" Jack retorted.

Tanner reached in, wedged a shoulder under Jack's right arm and hauled him out of the chopper. His knees immediately buckled, and Vince stepped up, supporting him on the other side.

"In a place like Stone Creek," Tanner replied, "everybody helps out."